EXPOSING HIDDEN WORKS OF DARKNESS

THE WISE MAN AND THE WARRIOR BOOK 5

L.A. GOODYEAR

Publishing Coordinator – Sharon Kizziah-Holmes
Cover Design – Jaycee DeLorenzo

Paperback-Press
an imprint of A & S Publishing
Paperback Press, LLC

ISBN -13: 978-1-964559-95-7

DEDICATION

Book 5 - never thought we'd get this far. When I started this tale, it was a retreat from the rejection of real life, the failure of the marriage that had come to define me over nearly four decades dissolved into nothingness. What was left? My imagination put together a fantasy that appealed to me, when life no longer did. I dove into the story, writing until exhausted.

Then the means to publish came about. My energy was redirected to that end, the content reorganized into the book series it has since become. Some of this book originated in the massive initial effort, then it was later completed, after a lengthy hiatus. Seven years have passed since the divorce finalized. A beautiful fantasy remains nothing more than fiction. I am still broken.

Christ is my only hope, my only intimate companion. He is coming for His Bride momentarily, the reason I'm surprised to have gotten this far in my publishing adventure. I believe, have to believe that hope does not disappoint. The apostle Paul was convinced it won't. I don't think I've borne much fruit to my Lord Jesus, but James said the fruit of some follow after them and cannot be hidden.

Therefore, I dedicate Book 5, *Exposing Hidden Works of Darkness*, to the Tribulation saints who will see these things and cleave to the God of my salvation - and theirs. Not just the 144,000 sealed Jewish witnesses entrusted with the gospel, but the countless others, both Jews and Gentiles, who come to realize Christ Jesus is *the* way, *the* truth and *the only life worth pursuing!* He is the pearl of great price that costs everything, the One many of you will prove the price is worth paying. I hope my story will drive home how you were loved before you knew it!

-Larry

ACKNOWLEDGMENTS

Paperback Press' proprietor **Sharon Kizziah-Holmes** works magic to get my stories in print, or so it seems to me! I am a published author because of her. That's no exaggeration. I'm not a household name yet, but the finished works my readers can hold in their hands are in no way inferior to products sold in bookstores everywhere and compare favorably to many of them. Her expertise gives my works that polish! Thanks again, Sharon.

Jaycee DeLorenzo made this cover. It's remarkable, calling to mind the pillar of fire scripture described going before the children of Israel as they followed it toward the promised land. It's the resemblance I was going for! Whatever I ask of her, she rises to the occasion every time. I highly recommend her Sweet 'n Spicy Designs to anyone needing cover art.

My niece **Kimberly** took on the task of editing. It's tedious work I can't do without, but she did it, despite holding a full-time job. In her shoes, I wouldn't have the energy. Thanks so much, Kim!

My **mom** is still cheering me on. Can't let her down! She is the inspiration for Ruth in my ongoing story, if you've wondered. It wouldn't have come this far without her encouragement. Turning a daydream into print others can enjoy is a lot of work; it requires motivation and exhortation that can only come from outside one's self. She is a dependable source of the latter.

As for motivation... If making money was the goal, my publishing adventure has been a colossal failure, so far. Continuing on this track would be utter folly, but there's much more to it than a hope of profit. The daydream may be therapeutic for me, but it doesn't need to be published to accomplish that goal. Keeping it to myself would actually avoid risk, since anything going public inevitably draws trolls!

God has given me the heart to share what is in me with strangers, in spite of the risk. You can't touch others when you remain out of reach yourself. Facades are a natural defense people hide behind, but this is their great failing. Ephesians tells us to put on the whole armor of God instead, making us mobile, enabling us to go to the hurting and comfort them wherever we find them. I hope my writings will comfort someone out there. Even though it's fiction, the God of the Bible portrayed in it is not. He is the remedy for every affliction, now more than ever!

Jesus Christ declared *"I am come that you have life, and that more abundantly."* If He was talking about this current life, His words were effectively a curse, but since we are already alive, He has to be referring to the life that comes after He resurrects us. This life is nothing more than a seed, so take heed how you plant it. There are a lot of fruitless trees out there. What's the appeal in becoming firewood?

CHAPTER 1

L aurie asked to stay over, so she and Emily were with Erin and Allen at the house. Erin wanted some time in the pool and informed him he did, too. He didn't know that, but was told they could use some exercise after such a lazy day! Laurie was all for it, wanting to show Emily the Allen dunk.

He tensed at the mention of it.

Erin noticed. She moved up against him, took his face in her hands, and planted such a kiss on him it curled his toes! "Don't you know by now you're safe with us, Sweet Talker? We'll play with you, but that's all."

"Said the shark to the tuna," he mumbled, though he couldn't suppress a grin.

There was a round of laughter as Erin led him off to change. He found no way to get out of it. The girls were already in the pool when they arrived. As the couple got in, a conspiratorial look passed between them.

"Okay," Emily said. "Laurie told me how Mom made you so nervous about getting dunked, then how she and

Heidi tossed you around the pool. We don't want you to be nervous about what *might* happen, Dad."

"That's right," Laurie assured him seriously, "so we've come up with a plan to help settle your mind. Will you help us, Mom?"

He thought he saw a smile on Erin's face as he turned toward her. He couldn't be sure; it vanished before he got a good look.

"If it will quell his nerves, I'm all for it! What do you two have in mind?"

The next thing he knew, his body was hoisted high over their heads.

"H-hey!" he hollered.

Someone announced, "Count of three," then he began to swing forward and back to counting. On three, he *flew* through the air into deeper water, hearing laughter cutting off as he went under. It was still present when he recovered to reach the surface.

"How was that supposed to help me?" he demanded.

Erin shook her head, "Now you don't have to wonder what might happen to you. It already did!"

Their giggles put a grin on his disbelieving face. "That's some logic! Did you get the desire to dunk me out of your system?"

Exchanging a look, they nodded.

"For now," Erin grinned wolfishly. "We're ornery. We can't help it, but we're not going to make you afraid of us, either."

Making his way back to them, he replied, "I'm ornery too, but outnumbered as I am, I don't think I'll push my luck... not right now, anyway."

He was wrapped in a three-way hug and kissed hard on the mouth by Erin. Giving him time to catch his breath, she challenged the others to a three-lap race. He was directed to declare the winner! It ended up very close. The slender Ukrainian edged out the others to win. Erin was second, right behind her. With her short limbs and robust build creating drag, he thought Laurie made an impressive showing, anyway. She was two or three seconds behind Erin.

When Laurie wanted to show Emily the Allen dunk, Erin called out sharply, "Hey!" She stalked toward them, a stern look on her features. No one knew what brought it on, so they just watched as she came to him, then turned to grin. "The line starts behind *me*, girls!"

It cracked them up. No one argued the point.

It was as big a hit as it had been with Laurie and Heidi. Emily loved it! When he began to tire, Erin pulled him aside, instructing the girls to practice on each other so he could rest. Laurie told Emily it was fun, but in her opinion, no one made it as much fun as Dad! This put a surprised little smile on his face, which in turn brought a smile from Erin.

She leaned close to whisper, "Why are you surprised, love? She may be grown, but for the first time in her life she can remember, her dad is playing with her. She's not too old to enjoy that!"

The insight gave him a sense of satisfaction as he considered it. They lingered in the pool for a good while, making human statues, splashing, even having a chicken fight at one point!

When they decided to call it a night, he got hugs and a kiss on the cheek from both girls, with thanks for all the fun. The couple said good night and hit the showers. Exhausted, he wrapped his arms around Erin as she snuggled up to him. He was out before he knew it.

Teasing woke him the next morning. It became unbearable when his attempts to take control failed, but she made sure he didn't have to endure it for long! When it was over, she caught him off-guard with a question, amidst more kisses.

"Sweet Talker, I *love* overwhelming you with

affection. It is hugely satisfying to hold you down and get the best of you. I can't tell you how much! It's almost like I'm forcing you, though, when I'm so intense. How does it make you feel?"

He grinned up at her. "That seems like an odd question to ask, at this point. Is something bothering you?"

"Well, when it seems like I'm taking any choice away from you... I just don't want you to resent it." She was earnest. "Do you?"

"Not in the slightest," he emphasized. "Erin, you make me feel loved and wanted, more than I thought anyone ever could! Jesus is the Great Physician. He prescribed you for me, remember?"

It got him a bright smile.

"You're not raping me, honey. There is nothing selfish or hurtful in how you handle me. You take my breath away, but all the while, you gauge the effect you're having, adjusting your actions to increase my pleasure. That's very *un*selfish of you.

"Besides, I love how you overpower me! Your forcefulness makes me feel desirable, even if I don't understand why you think I am. All I ask is that you let me show you some appreciation, too -- *before* you drain all my energy!"

She broke into laughter, acknowledging she could do that, with some effort.

He stroked her hair as he admired her. "You are so beautiful! Overwhelm me to your heart's content, but I challenge you to let me show you some affection before you finish me off. You're not afraid of what might happen, are you?"

"Oh, ho!" her eyes widened, the wolfish grin appearing above him, "A challenge, eh? I can take anything *you* can dish out, dear, turning the tables anytime I want! Nothing will thrill me more than proving it again and again. I'm always going to win, you know." Another hard kiss emphasized her point.

"I know you will," he agreed, "yet the funny thing is I'm never going to lose, since I win when you win!"

"Very shrewd," she commended him, then covered his face in kisses before letting him up with a laugh. "My wise man!"

He dried his face with the blanket. "Your wise soggy man, you mean."

That only brought more laughter.

CHAPTER 2

Their conference call that morning was blessed. The new families were on the line in force, every last member. Introductions were made with Heidi. They studied a passage from the book of Acts and prayed together, then Allen asked if anyone had questions, comments or thoughts to share.

The tall redhead spoke up. "Dad, TV programs are increasingly speculating about things like Bigfoot, Mothman and the Loch Ness monster. Is all that stuff imaginary? I don't know what to think. Does the Bible speak of any of it? What do you think?"

There were a couple of chuckles, but most just listened.

"Wow, Heidi, that's a big question without a simple answer. It will take time to give you my best response. I'm not sure everyone here would be well served by going into it. No, I don't think it's imaginary. Some scripture may lay groundwork for it, depending on perspective. It might be better to cover it with you when we return home."

Their girls were present, having stayed overnight. Fran, Denise, Andrew and Dani had returned to the house to join them.

Dani shivered, "Allen, I think we *need* to hear this. I'm not sure if the Holy Spirit is impressing me with it, or if it's just me. My brother and I saw Bigfoot when we were kids. We never forgot!"

She was plainly uncomfortable and those present perked up. Emily took her hand as Erin inquired softly, "What happened?"

Dani drew a deep breath. "We grew up outside Redding, here in northern California. I was thirteen at the time. Mom was sick, but her cancer had not yet been diagnosed. Dad took her to the doctor.

"Being four years older than my brother, I was left home to watch him. Not having close neighbors, our house was secluded, with deep woods behind it. The backyard was fenced in, with a swing set. We decided to go out and swing.

"We did, until we saw something squatting in a big tree outside the fence. It was rock-still, looking a bit like a gorilla at first. Shadows kept us from getting a good look, so we stopped swinging to move closer. Nothing in the woods frightened us before. We were curious. When we neared the back fence, we got the creeps and stopped.

"When the breeze shifted, we got a whiff of it and nearly gagged. It smelled like something dead and rotting! Raising its head then, we saw glowing red eyes. It was watching us the whole time. Something about those eyes seemed to shout hatred toward us! We turned and fled for the house in a panic. I glanced over my shoulder, got a good look as it dropped out of the tree and stepped over the 5-foot tall fence effortlessly. It was taller than our swing set, and it was pursuing us."

"We got in the back door, slammed and locked it, then something hit it so hard the house shook! I jammed a chair under the knob, then we ducked down, hearing huffing noises. That faded after a minute. I risked looking out a back window. It was standing by the swing, looking directly at me! It was ugly and *evil*; no way was it an ape.

"It swung a huge arm violently to cave in one end of the swing set, then turned and walked away without looking back. I watched it go, making my brother stay down until it was gone.

"We told Mom and Dad about it when they got home. They looked at the swing set, puzzled about the damage, but I don't think what we told them registered. Mom had been diagnosed with breast cancer. They were in shock, and so were we at the news. Dad put the house up for sale, moving us to stay with family in L.A. the same week so Mom could get treatment.

"My brother shook it off better than I did, but he never looked it full in the face. No animal ever looked at me that way! It was intelligent and *wanted* to kill us; it left no doubt in my mind.

"Maybe this isn't the right time to talk about it, Allen, but if you can shed any light on that *thing*, I need to hear it. It kind of messed me up, even though it happened nearly twenty years ago." The white knuckles of her hand grasping Emily's bore witness to the disturbance she felt.

Erin exchanged a look with him, and they nodded together. "Okay. This just went from an idle question to an issue troubling one of us. That makes it important, urgent. Dani, we'll discuss this today. I can't prove most of what I'll tell you, but perhaps what I believe God has revealed to me can set your mind at ease and give you peace. That makes it worth the risk of looking like a fool, sister."

"Thank you," she replied.

He nodded. "How about we start this after lunch? The subject could take hours. Heidi, is that okay with you? I imagine you'll want to plug in your phone for this."

"I look forward to it, even have a headset," she

chuckled. "What time?"

"How many are interested in this?" Erin broke in.

'Me' was uttered copiously, swamping the connection, resulting in laughter.

"Love, I think you have a seriously intrigued audience!"

Hans stated, "Normally, I'd consider this kind of talk nonsense, but not after yesterday, not coming from you, Allen. It has been proven to me that you have a handle on things I can no longer deny or dismiss. I will hear you out! Is this something that will frighten our kids?"

A couple of groans indicated disappointment at the prospect of being excluded.

"Good question! No, I don't think so. If what Dani just shared didn't scare them, I think they'll be okay. No matter how weird things get, there is reassurance in hearing none of it escapes God's notice. His sovereignty and commitment to us in Christ will keep us in peace and safety."

Distinct sighs of relief put a smile on his face.

"Okay, how about 2:00 p.m.? That gives us time to eat, while anyone who wants to join us will be freed from the hassle of holding a phone to his ear. Heidi, sorry I can't help you there."

"I have my headset, Dad. I'm looking forward to it!"

In the three hours beforehand, Erin coordinated takeout and readied snacks for whoever might show up. She expected a full house. It turned out she was right! Ted wanted to record the discussion for Eli. Though the college freshman couldn't attend, he was very interested. Allen said it was okay. In his opinion, their conversation was unlikely to mesh with university perspectives!

When all were gathered, they bowed their heads to pray. Acknowledging God's sovereignty and omniscience, Allen asked for peace to cover them and that He would keep them from error and deception, revealing truth as He saw fit. Nothing spoken of today would ever surpass what Jesus did at the cross for them or the hope He provided by His resurrection! In the light of His gospel, they would attempt to reveal the hidden works of darkness brought about by Satan's infestation of this planet and his war against truth. May the light of truth shine in them as they walk in it and remain faithful!

CHAPTER 3

S uch peace settled over the reception room where they were gathered that everyone heaved a sigh of relief. Grins lit up the room.

Andrew chuckled, "To have the Lord honor us with His presence like this... That's reason enough for being here!"

Nods and 'amens' affirmed his statement.

Allen nodded. "I'm going to reference some ancient documents in the course of this discussion," he prefaced. "While I don't give them equal standing with scripture, I consider them trustworthy because scripture references them. It degrades scripture to view this as accidental. The book of Hebrews specifically states that *all* scripture is God-breathed, so even referenced texts are mentioned for a purpose.

"Have you heard of the Dead Sea scrolls?"

Most indicated they had.

"I believe their preservation was divinely orchestrated, God's version of a time capsule, if you will. Documents from ancient Israel were preserved after its destruction, unedited and unaltered by intervening generations. They were discovered in 1947, one year before modern Israel's establishment. It took two years to translate them, which worked out perfectly, since the nation's first year was consumed in a fight for survival against hostile neighbors. Who could time it so precisely but God?"

Heads shook in wonder.

"Among those documents was the Book of Enoch. It is referenced in scripture by the Apostle Peter, and it is outright quoted in Jude. The Coptic Church of Ethiopia and Egypt has a version of it, but the two do not compare. Their version has been corrupted over the centuries. Satan corrupts human memory subtly whenever he can, because truth rarely serves his purposes. Knowing this, God preserves truth for our benefit. We choose which to believe.

"Genesis chapter six, the first four verses, declares the advent of giants and how they came to exist. It says *the sons of God* went in to the daughters of men so they conceived, plainly indicating they had sex. The term translated as *'sons of God'* occurs four times in scripture, always referring to angels.

"It was an act of angelic rebellion against God, as it broke one of the laws of creation. Every mortal creature is to bring forth offspring after its own kind. Since immortal angels are not designed to reproduce in their own form, the transgressors hijacked the reproductive capabilities of mankind."

"God permitted this?!" Teresa exclaimed.

Expressions indicated a number of those present were having difficulty digesting what he told them.

"God *judges* sin, sister. That means He has to let it be committed, to some extent. If He prevented it, there would be no free will. He limits it at times, when He perceives the damage it initiates will be too harmful, but reserves the right to judge after the fact."

Alissa inquired in a forlorn voice, "Were the women forced against their will?"

His voice and countenance softened. "There is no indication that happened. In fact, it seems some women actually *enticed* those beings."

Her features expressed distaste.

"Angels can take any physical form they choose. If a man could choose his appearance, we'd all be handsome, strapping, virile young men, wouldn't we? Especially if our primary interest is attracting female attention!"

The observation brought chuckles.

"Taking on those forms, spiritual beings abruptly experienced a human sex drive unfamiliar to them, nearly uncontrollable. God never intended to place them in that position. There are always some women around who are willing to capitalize on a situation like that! These men were unlike any they had seen, irresistible, a prize catch for a husband.

"Their children surpassed other women's children in every measurable way. What parent *wouldn't* be proud? Their mates taught them knowledge of the divine realm, ways to do things other people couldn't do. Witchcraft began with those women, taught them by illicit husbands in full-blown rebellion against God."

Carol spoke, "What madness! It couldn't last. The world would have been destroyed!"

"It almost was. Remember why God sent the flood? *'All flesh had corrupted its way on the earth.'* A gene had been introduced into humanity that was never meant to interact with life here, perverting everything it touched. The giants were lawless, spreading their perverted seed indiscriminately across a myriad of creatures through bestial acts. Beast-man hybrids proliferated as a result. The seed carried with it a desire to consume living flesh and drink blood, too!

"God permitted it to continue long enough for all to

see where it was going, then washed the earth clean, starting over through Noah's obedience. Enoch wrote that two hundred angels conspired to physically violate humanity. Though their monstrous corrupted offspring were destroyed, the flood could not touch the rebellious angels who initiated the mess.

"The world was brought to the brink of destruction through their meddling in just a few centuries. What was to prevent them from doing it again? I believe their purpose was twofold. First, they wanted to pollute the line of the woman's Seed destined to crush the serpent's head. If the prophecy in Eden might be foiled, they reasoned Jesus couldn't be born incorruptible to atone for humanity's sins. God could not permit that! Second, if only a third of the angels rebelled against God, they are badly outnumbered, unless they can breed reinforcements for their final battle!"

"That actually makes sense, tactically speaking," Pam observed.

"To an intellect flawed enough to rebel against God in the first place, it doesn't seem like a reach, I'm guessing. Satan had nothing more to lose by trying! Of those two hundred, nearly all were imprisoned in the bottomless pit.

"A few were designated as examples. Their crimes were so atrocious they were shackled in chains of darkness, buried alive in deep places of the earth and covered over with sharp stones to prevent their escape. They were considered too dangerous to be released before being transferred to the lake of fire!"

"That's crazy!" Erik gasped.

Allen shook his head, "Nuh-uh. What's crazy is there are people actively trying to dig them out!"

Shocked disbelief was mirrored on every face.

"Are you serious? Who would be so stupid?" Conrad wanted to know.

"Anyone looking for power, regardless of the cost," Heidi announced calmly.

Several felt a chill at the thought.

"I watched it on a National Geographic program, folks. A submerged cave under a mountain in Mexico is being pumped out 24/7 to be explored by scientists. Gigantic crystals are jumbled throughout it, "sharp stones." The temperature and humidity make it necessary to wear protective body suits with portable oxygen tanks. Even then, they can only bear ten minutes before they have to retreat and cool down!

"They claim to be "looking for life," making a show of scraping surfaces to find microscopic organisms, but their dogged determination to explore the whole place belies what they say. They were excited when they found an opening going deeper, though their suits couldn't protect them long enough to explore it safely. I expect they are constructing better gear for the descent now. Some of the most technical equipment they are using is supplied by NASA."

"Then there is *no way* they are simply exploring for micro-organisms," Hans stated.

Ted concurred, "You're right. They're looking to make first contact, or at least find evidence alien life has been there."

"Man won't manage to break '*everlasting chains of darkness*' to set the prisoners free, but they might succeed in making contact," Allen postulated. "The thing is, if they are televising what they are doing in this instance, how many other such projects are underway elsewhere, without our knowledge? There's no doubt in my mind they will get more than they bargained for, if they succeed!"

Heads nodded in agreement.

"Anyway, of the two hundred renegade angels, three have been permitted freedom to continue what they were doing."

Several objected.

"You've got to be kidding!" Carlos blurted out. "*Why*

would God allow that?"

"Because the time when He will preside to judge and put away sin hasn't arrived yet. The handful in chains are locked away as an example of God's displeasure, also for the danger they pose to the human race.

"Those in the bottomless pit are simply detained from their intentions to prevent the planet from being overrun too soon. There is an appointed time when it will happen, the Great Tribulation, during which the pit will be opened. Don't worry! Jesus will meet us in the air to take us home before it takes place."

CHAPTER 4

He gave it a moment to sink in, then decided to change perspective. "Has anyone tried to envision eternity? It's hard to do. We have no frame of reference. Throughout our lives, time is passing. Some have tried to codify 'eternity past' or 'eternity future' to get a handle on it. It doesn't work. God says He inhabits eternity, which means He fills it. It's another way of expressing how limitless He is.

"That's why He can say He has declared the end from the beginning. What He says defines *both*. In Eden, at man's fall into sin, God declared the Seed of the woman would redeem us. For us it was a prophecy, but for Him, it was a done deal as soon as He declared it!

"The same applies to the angelic revolt. God declared it before it happened, how many would rebel, and the outcome from an eternal perspective. In His eyes, it is finished! That's why Jesus could say He saw Satan fall like lightning from heaven. He sees the end of a matter from the beginning of time. The book of Job says Satan presented himself before God, so it had not happened yet. The book of Revelation places the event as yet to come. Jesus also calls him the ruler of this age. He would have no power, if it wasn't granted to him from above for the time being.

"The revolt begins in heaven, but it will culminate on Earth at the battle of Armageddon. Michael and the angels with him will defeat Satan's angelic forces in the heavens. The defeated foe will be hurled to the earth, where they will ally with the corrupted flesh they spawned to make a last stand, bolstered by the multitude of humanity who have rejected the grace of God in Christ Jesus. Jesus Himself will slay them all with a word from His mouth. There won't even be a battle, not really!"

"That starts the millennial reign, right?" Fran asked.

"You got it! The lake of fire will be opened, into which the Antichrist and False Prophet will be cast alive. Satan will be bound and imprisoned in the bottomless pit for a thousand years, his angelic troops cast into the lake of fire with the demons that followed them. Peace will reign on earth during that time, an enforced peace that only the Prince of Peace could bring. We will reign with Him, by the way."

A hand shot up. It was Laurie's. A few chuckled, but a couple of other hands went up, as well. He called on Laurie.

"What will it be like, reigning with Him? Does the Bible say, or is there anything you can tell us, Dad?"

"The Bible doesn't define it in detail. I may have some insight, but I'd rather not go into it here. We already have enough to talk about for this session, okay?" She nodded.

Erik's hand was next. "Allen, are ghosts real?" He received irritated looks from several, including his family.

He smiled at him. "Not in the traditional sense, Erik, but in a way, demons are ghosts. I'm getting to that; you're just a little bit ahead of me." He nodded and grinned, vindicated.

Juanita got his attention, "So if I understand you right, Mr. Allen, you are saying that demons and fallen angels are not the same thing, yes?"

"That's right, Juanita. Fallen angels initiated a lineage of demons. When they had children, they petitioned God that their kids would be immortal, as they were. God refused their request, including His edict in scripture. *'My spirit* (literally breath) *shall not always strive* (or abide) *with man; for his days shall be 120 years.'*

"In the context, He is speaking of the giants, a new kind of being. Men and women were living 900 years plus at the time! Giant life expectancy was only granted a fraction of that time. You reckon they were jealous of our puny ancestors?"

Wide-eyed nods answered him.

"Jealous, volatile, pleasure-seeking lawless giants who were accountable to *no one* would have been a terror on the earth in those days.

"When they died, the *holy* angels who serve God asked where their spirits should be held until the Day of Judgment. Human spirits were gathered and held under the earth, the wicked in one place, the righteous in another. Jesus relocated the latter to a place He called Paradise after His crucifixion.

"No place was appointed for the giants to rest. God called them Wicked, Demons, unclean spirits doomed to wander the surface of the earth they had abused, but now were unable to touch. They could watch the living, yet were unable to indulge in physical pleasures like before. It gave them cause for jealousy all over again!

"They weren't entirely powerless, though. With nothing else to do, they began to explore their abilities as spirits. Learning they could project thoughts into the minds of the living, they could create chaos and disorder, sometimes even manipulate people to sin for their own entertainment. It proved God's names for them were accurate! They were as wicked as ever. Sin opened the living up to cohabitation or infestation by demons who never tire of tormenting their hosts.

"Only God limited the madness. Nine-tenths of all demons at the time of the flood, including the spirits of beast-men the giants sired, were sealed up in the bottomless pit with the bulk of the fallen angels who started all this mess. They are locked away until the pit is opened during the Tribulation. One-tenth remained to wander the earth.

"Since the time of the flood, neither they nor the remaining three angelic subversives have been idle. More giants have been spawned. Og, King of Bashan, and Goliath are the most well-known, but there were many more. The Book of Jasher holds eyewitness accounts of beast-man hybrids as well. The Bible mentions "lion-like men of Moab" killed by David's elite mighty men. All these oddities arose *after* the flood."

Danielle gestured, so he stopped. "Allen, this is fascinating, but how does it tie into what I saw? That *thing* wasn't part beast, part man. It was an intelligent, violent *monster* I knew wanted to kill my brother and me! It could have broken into the house, but it ran away. It *was* big, maybe like a giant, but it was wild, not human. What was it? Why did it stop?"

He felt a pang of sympathy. "I really am getting to it, sis, but without laying all this background, the answer sounds like pure science fiction. It's not! There is a sound basis for all of this, much of which is indicated in scripture. That's important, because there is no reassurance without knowing God is aware of what is happening and is in control of the outcome.

"I'm only expounding on these things so you can have that comfort and reassurance. You know me! Would I spout so-called 'knowledge' for no reason, just in an effort to impress you? I hope you know me better than that."

She colored, a little smile evident. "I do. I just got

caught up in all this forbidden history, couldn't see how it connected to my experience. None of us would respect you if you were a blowhard! I'll try to be more patient."

"I'll try to make it worth your wait."

Laurie put an arm around her shoulders. It made him smile. Erin laid a hand on his knee and gave him a smile of encouragement.

"Did y'all know God has a government in the heavens for this world's operation, similar to how each nation has a government?"

There were a few smiles and nods, but most seemed surprised.

"It's true. Each nation has a Prince, or principality, who stands over it to give an account before God. Scripture says the archangel Michael is Israel's Prince.

"There is corruption in that government, too, due to Lucifer's rebellion. The Prince of Persia fought a holy angel to prevent him from reaching Daniel with a message from God's throne. Daniel lived in Persia, remember? The message was delayed for three weeks until Michael aided the messenger. It didn't end the battle. The messenger said another Prince was coming to help the wicked Prince of Persia!

"This kind of stuff is ongoing in the heavenlies. The war in the heavens until Satan is cast down to earth sounds like one pitched battle. Many overlook it is labeled a *war*. The indications are that the war started when the serpent in Eden deceived Eve and has been underway ever since!

"It will continue until Jesus embarks toward earth to set up His kingdom. Michael's forces will unseat those wicked powers in the heavenlies, who will then be cast down to earth so a path is cleared for Jesus' approach!"

CHAPTER 5

Tom let out a low whistle, "So that's how it all fits! I never heard it put together that way. It makes sense!"

Ted and Liz were nodding, "Yes, it does, more than it ever did before," he agreed. "Satan will try to shake off his defeat, marshaling all his forces to make his greatest stand at Megiddo. He won't realize how screwed he is! He will expect another conflict with Michael, but when Jesus Himself appears with us and all His angels at His back, a single word from our King will dash all his hopes!"

Grins appeared on every face.

"Yep," Allen chuckled, "It's fun to anticipate, isn't it?"

Nods and chuckles answered him.

"There is much more to divine government than Princes, though. There are angels assigned responsibility for upholding natural laws governing this world, more than I am aware of or understand."

"For example, angels govern the winds, at least four of them. There may be more. I'm pretty sure the Lord showed me there is one maintaining Earth's magnetic field. Gravity, planetary orbits, tectonic activity, etc.; everything we take for granted is maintained through angelic caretakers.

"Enoch referred to these beings collectively as the Watchers. It's an apt name, as they watch to see how the Lord fulfills the purposes for which He created us! They are accountable to God as they carry out their duties. Remember, not all are honest or trustworthy, but nothing they do is hidden from Him, either. The two hundred who set forth to multiply and produce offspring abandoned their posts, for they were Watchers, too. Think of them as the vanguard of the mutiny against God.

"They are unbelievably powerful from our point of view, but compared to their Maker, all of them combined are as nothing. He is matchless! As they gloried in their own abilities, they forgot Who gave them such power. He gave them life and could withdraw it, just as easily!

"Most of the Watchers have been faithful. Beholding God in all His glory, they have not turned away. The wickedness of the unfaithful irks them, reflects on them all. As a result, they are very zealous servants of our God! Not much of their workings and decisions are revealed to us, but one specific act of theirs is laid out in detail in scripture."

Opening his Bible to chapter four of Daniel, he handed it to Erin, asking her to read two verses, then pass it on. Each read two verses until Nebuchadnezzar's tale was complete. By the time it was finished, all not previously familiar with the tale were shocked!

"That really happened, Allen?" Alissa asked timidly.

"It's in scripture, sweetie," he told her, "Written by the hated king who burned Solomon's Temple and carried Judah away into captivity. It never would have been included in Jewish scripture, if it wasn't true. What happened to the king of the known world at the time was the edict of the Watchers, not specifically God's. He was aware of it, but *they* handled it in the course of their administration. It was in their jurisdiction.

"Nothing else like this is in the Bible, but no one was ever given insight into the workings of Heaven like Daniel was. Nebuchadnezzar was taught a lesson, mission accomplished. *Why* was it recorded for us?"

"Wasn't it a lesson against pride?" Denise asked.

"Yes, it was. The Bible is very clear about the dangers of pride, but never hints at consequences like this, other than in this passage. Why record a one-time event of such a peculiar nature?"

Silence was the response until Andrew spoke in a low tone, "Maybe it wasn't a one-time event. Oooh, I wish I hadn't said that! It's giving me goosebumps."

Shivers accompanied several 'me, too' comments.

"That's the conclusion I arrived at, too. The same Watchers who issued the edict are still in power, ageless, immortal. The king of the earth was temporarily sentenced to his fate by these beings. The ancient pre-flood giants were known as kings of the earth, by the way.

"I can't prove it, so time will have to tell if I'm on the right track. I think giants have multiplied, much more than we know. To keep them in check, the Watchers have done something similar to them in recent times. They have been driven away from us, their minds reduced to bestial urges for our protection. Their comprehension is still far above any animal's, though, and their hatred toward us is in no way diminished.

"The number of encounters has increased for two reasons. Mankind has multiplied to such an extent that we are *everywhere*, so driving them from us has become problematic. Where can they go, to get away from us? Also, I think they know the time of lawlessness is drawing near, *their* time. II Thessalonians calls Antichrist '*the lawless one.*' The time of Tribulation is the time of lawlessness. Paul called it a mystery. As their time gets closer, they are getting excited, fighting the constraints placed on them!"

He turned toward Dani. "It didn't break into the house because it was not *permitted* to. Certain unwritten laws prevent it from crossing a threshold, uninvited. No animal can observe such a law, but it was under restraint, even if you couldn't tell. Likewise, it wasn't permitted to catch you outside. The hate and evil intent you saw in its features was real, but you were under protection, though you didn't know at the time. It couldn't wait around for you to come out, because it was *driven away* against its will."

She heaved a sigh of relief. "So we were never really in danger."

"I wouldn't go that far," he shook his head. "If you hadn't run for the house, shut and locked the door, it might have been allowed to take you. Strange things happen in this world! I don't pretend to understand all the unwritten laws governing them.

"Let's just say you were *helped* to get away. You were not left alone to face the danger. Angels do not work independently of God in safeguarding us, so we can all thank Him for getting you clear!"

"He helped us before we knew Him," she pondered with a smile. "I like that!"

"Why hasn't anyone killed one?" Hans wondered.

"How do you know they haven't?" Allen countered. "There are rumors it has happened. I don't trust rumors, but I can see how quickly it could be covered up. People disappear all the time, and dead men tell no tales. Giant bones have been dug up many times over the past century, but governments seize them, and they almost *always* disappear. Giant remains wreak havoc with the deception of evolution.

"As far as Bigfoot is concerned, he's tough to find. Native Americans believe he is an evil spirit, have contended so for centuries. Their beliefs are pagan and superstitious, but something led them to that conclusion. They are some of the best trackers the world has ever seen, but the "Wild Man," as they called him, would leave tracks that would suddenly disappear without a trace. It happened many times.

"If they are sired by fallen angels, perhaps they have the ability to temporarily step into the fringes of the spiritual realm. To those who cannot follow, they would seem to disappear. Their mortality might weigh heavily on them there, which could account for the stench of death they exude and the Bible's description that they are unclean. It might also explain how they usually see us before we detect them. That stood out as odd in the sightings I've read about.

"It's also been postulated they can *confuse* people. Numerous accounts support the idea. God is not the author of confusion, we are assured in scripture, but if He considers it worth pointing out, the implication is some *do* author confusion."

He homed in on Erik, who brightened when he realized it. "You asked about ghosts. Human ghosts, no, but spirits remaining from corrupted flesh, giants and beastmen – *absolutely*. They are very real. They love to impersonate dead individuals, deceiving the gullible. Since they observed them in life, they can be convincing impostors, too.

"They can't read our minds, but they are marvelous at interpreting body language, having observed us for millennia, so they can intuit what we are thinking so well it seems supernatural. It's why so many people believe in ghosts.

"It's not the only reason, though. A curious term occurs in scripture that goes like this, 'the stones bear witness.' God told Cain the earth cried out for the blood of his brother, whom he murdered. Again, I have a theory I can't prove. Do you want to hear it?"

He nodded quickly, excited Allen was addressing what his family had dismissed. They seemed intrigued, too.

"Okay, based on what I've read in scripture, I believe the earth itself has a memory. That's how it can bear witness to God concerning what has taken place upon it. Like an old vinyl record or a modern CD, it manifests what has been impressed on it. The earth also spins on its axis, sometimes visibly or audibly manifesting what has passed in a specific location.

"In those cases, it replays past moments or events in a way that seems ethereal to us, ghostly. Those moments take no notice of anyone present now, because it's nothing more than a recording. The people in them are shadows of people long gone, that's all. There is nothing demonic or evil working, but for the living, it can be disquieting, like living too close to an airport. Strong emotion, or perhaps sin, seems to leave the strongest imprints. Reenactments would certainly stress an unprepared observer."

"You're describing hauntings!" the youngster burst forth in excitement.

CHAPTER 6

"**S**ometimes, that's all there is to it," he qualified. "Sometimes demons terrorize people. They hate the living! Many have nothing better to do. It amuses them to frighten or hurt folks."

"You said earlier that demons and those three angels have not been idle since the flood," Liz reminded him. She looked at Ted, then back. "We've never heard any of this stuff before, yet enough scripture leaves the possibility open that we're not dismissing it outright. Before yesterday, we would have! If I understand you right, those angels are still fathering giants, but their interaction with us is being prevented by the administrators of God's divine government, these 'Watchers.'"

He nodded.

She continued, "Okay. Only three angels are on it, but they've had thousands of years to work. Even if giants are mortal, there could be a serious population of them by now!"

He nodded emphatically.

"You just said many of the demons have nothing better to do than frighten or injure people. My question is this: if others have found something better to do, what is it?"

"Liz, you just asked the prize question! Now I'll ask you one. What would disembodied ghosts of notoriously sensual beings who are unable to find rest want, more than anything else?"

She looked at him blankly.

Guillermo supplied a response, "New bodies, so they could *feel* again."

Andrew shook his head, "Thanks, Gui. Now *you're* giving me the shivers!"

The younger man shrugged, "It seemed obvious to me."

Heidi's voice was on speakerphone, "They already inhabit people, experiencing feelings through the host. I'm proof some hosts welcome them! What more could they want?"

Allen replied, "They desire freedom to do as they please, when they please, without risk their host might get in the way... like you did."

She exclaimed "Ooh!"

"They *despise* their hosts. They long for the day when they can afford to ruin or kill that individual. They are ingrates! A host isn't appreciated, but resented in jealousy.

"They want bodies of their own, free of any other will but their own. I have no idea what lengths they have gone to obtain them. Truthfully, I don't want to know! God knows. That's good enough for me! They have probably received assistance from fallen angels in the heavenlies. Almost certainly, they have deceived and co-opted people to assist their quest, with promises of shared knowledge and power.

"Surely, you have all heard stories of alien abductions, experimentation, and cattle mutilations?"

There were some nods, but some snorts.

"Even dismissing ninety percent of those accounts, as with Bigfoot encounters, enough remain with evidence and credible witnesses to indicate some truth exists in them. Recognizing this, multiple governments have launched probes seeking the truth. They wouldn't if they didn't take it seriously."

There were nods and grunts of acknowledgment.

"Even if they find something, it's improbable they'll go public with the truth. Those in power prefer not to share knowledge with us. But enough is public knowledge to draw some conclusions."

His audience leaned forward.

"Demons have found some limited success in designing bodies to house them, temporarily. They are not strong or stable, but they are making progress. Scripture states *life* is in the blood. Cattle mutilations are commonly found with the blood missing completely. The 'aliens', who are really demons, are maintaining themselves in corporeal form at the expense of God's creation.

"Some of those claiming to have been abducted have been implanted with very real, yet unidentified, technology. Only lasers have worked to penetrate the devices, which still defy identification. One thing has been agreed upon, by those few doctors willing to speak of what they've found: they await a signal to transform the patient in some way at a cellular level. They cannot speculate what the transformation might look like. Some devices can't be removed because the patient's life signs destabilize when the attempt is made.

"Also, those visited by 'aliens' seem to be chosen at random, but once selected, they are usually revisited multiple times. There is one notable exception to this rule. Anyone who calls on the name of *Jesus* finds they rapidly withdraw and do not return! It kind of gives away their identity, don't you think?"

The room lit up with grins.

"Even 'aliens' know who He is and want no part of Him!"

"Heidi, have I answered your questions to your satisfaction, for the time being?"

She laughed, "Better than I expected, Dad. Thank you for taking me seriously!"

"Why wouldn't I? You're my girl!"

She giggled.

"How about you, Dani? Are you at peace now?"

She nodded, smiling. "For the first time ever, the memory doesn't make me tense. Even when I picture that hateful face, it's okay. I know it can't hurt me!"

Erin squeezed his knee and gave him a grin. It put a smile on his face.

"Other questions will arise, I'm sure," he told the group. "I don't always have answers, but I will always give you the very best I have. You are my family in Christ! If nothing else, Erin and I will pray with you. My advice is to file all this stuff away and focus on our Savior. We rely on Him to face each day, unlike the things we just talked about.

"I could be wrong in some of my conclusions. If I am, that's okay. I don't have to be right about everything, as long as I'm right with Him!"

Hans walked up to him and extended his hand.

Allen cocked his head questioningly, gazing with disdain at his limb.

Hans chuckled, spreading his arms.

"That's more like it!" Allen declared, embracing him.

His family was right behind him, smiling. Alissa giggled.

Erik commented, "You're gonna make a hugger of my dad yet!"

Grinning as they broke, Allen shook his head. "He isn't doing anything he doesn't want to do."

"That's true," Hans agreed. "I wasn't raised this way,

but... this kind of expression feels right, somehow. Son, I think Jesus is making a hugger of me now!

"Allen, my family means *everything* to me. They always have, yet you set the bar even higher, without realizing it. These people are no relation to you, yet you call them – *us* – your family in Christ, *and you mean it!*"

The room had gone silent, listening. Several faces bore tears, and heads nodded.

Hans went on, "You said something a while ago about risking looking like a fool, but you did it anyway, just to comfort one of us. That's love! I said it before, I'll say it again; we're with you, even if you mess up or get something wrong!"

The room broke into applause. Erin moved next to him, her arm going around his waist. Alissa hugged him with a grin. After a moment, Erik did, too. It took him a moment to find his voice.

"I'm glad, 'cause if I haven't messed up yet, I will. I can't help it!"

Erin pointed out, "You wouldn't be human if you didn't, love. Don't worry, I'll set you straight when you do!" The mischief in her eyes was unmistakable.

It made him laugh. His arm went around her shoulders and scrunched her to him. "I'll be a better man for it, too!"

She grinned.

Andrew stood before him, arms open wide, grinning as he awaited his hug.

He did the best he could, despite his girth.

"Did the goosebumps fade off, big fellow?"

He chuckled, "Mostly. I had no idea how the spiritual realm was organized, before today. Hearing it has intruded on us with malicious intent, though... That still creeps me out! I'm glad Jesus has a handle on it. It would be terrifying, otherwise."

"Everything covered today was just a rough outline of how things stand," Allen told him. "You wouldn't believe how far-reaching the spiritual conflict extends, brother. I only understand parts of it, as the Holy Spirit has revealed it to me. In studying scripture, my heart was moved for those who will come to faith in the dreadful time of Tribulation. I wanted to help them. However, we'll be with Christ then.

"I shared my desire with Him. He began to unveil prophetic scripture, also revealing details it doesn't directly address. I felt honored, but didn't understand why, if I wouldn't be present to see it fulfilled.

"He reminded me of my prayers. They pleased Him! If I would risk ridicule to write it down, it will bear witness to those faced with it in time to come, *that God is still in control!*"

"In days when terror runs rampant, that could be invaluable," Win interjected. "Are you writing, then?"

"Some. If it's all laughed at and scorned before it becomes useful, I'm concerned it will be discarded too soon to help anyone. Everyone's a critic, especially the religious."

Pam spoke, "How about this, then? Write it as fiction, not overtly intent on being taken seriously. If you wrote of a fictional relationship between characters you invent, what would prevent you from passing on truths you have learned in the course of their relationship?"

He looked at Erin. Both cracked up laughing.

"Boy, you *really* want us to write a book about relationships, don't you?" he observed, amused.

"Hey, I still think you should! It was a good idea. Do it for all of us girls," she cajoled them, smiling.

The couple shared how Emily wasn't waiting for a book, instead moving in to study them personally.

Pam got a good laugh about it! "Bold move!" she clapped Emily on the shoulder. "I like it!"

She directed her attention toward the couple with a smirk. "Parents have a responsibility to be role models, you know, even after the kids are grown. You might not see yourselves in that light, but you two are *worth* emulating, especially for those of us you led to Christ! Who else should we trust to show us how to live for Him? We could do a lot worse than learning how to care for one another by watching how you care for us and each other!"

"Whoa!" He was not expecting such a powerful argument.

Erin looked at him with a wry smile, "I think she's got us, Sweet Talker. We can't responsibly walk away from the needs of those we love, can we?"

"Of course not!" Pam grinned triumphantly.

"Okay, I guess we'll write a book. You honestly think someone will look at it?"

Now she seemed sympathetic, "Guys, I can't say what others will do, but I will. I think there'll be others, too. If *one more soul* comes to Christ because of the witness you put in print, won't it make the effort worthwhile?"

They couldn't deny what she said!

He advised Win, "Don't ever try to argue with this woman, my brother. You may *be* Win, but you won't win if you argue with her. That's experience talking," he glanced sideways toward Erin.

Both ladies laughed.

"I hear you," Win smiled, "but as much as I love her, she isn't perfect, either. What should I do when I know she's *wrong*?"

"Respectfully tell her why you disagree, then *drop it,* just listen. She deserves your honesty and will respect you for it. Present it to the Lord, who can put you in agreement with Him. She may be wrong, or you might be, but He *isn't,* so let Him do the convincing."

Win nodded. The ladies did, too.

He looked at Erin, "Sometimes He has a better way than either of us considered, when it comes down to it. If He's in charge, then we're united in following Him, right?"

Pam took her man's hand and winked at them. "See? That's the kind of thing you need to put in writing. It makes sense! In the heat of a moment, contending points of view could overlook sensibility. Besides, I was right this time, and I'm enjoying the moment!"

They all dissolved into laughter.

CHAPTER 7

C arol caught him with a question, "Allen, we've been taught men are to be the spiritual head of the household. Ultimately, they will stand before Jesus to be held responsible for decisions made. How do you reconcile your responsibility with your... unwillingness... to take a stand your wife finds disagreeable, should it ever happen?"

Silence dropped over the room. He knew it was a legitimate query of doctrine, but it sounded like his manhood was being challenged. Anger was palpable!

He chuckled to lighten the mood. "Sister, you have a knack for asking hard questions!"

She smiled, while angry looks were deflected toward him in curiosity.

"I have freely admitted my wife is stronger than I am. I'm proud of her in an odd way, I guess, but I'm not easy-going because she intimidates me. She doesn't. She chooses not to, knowing I couldn't live like that.

"You're right. As Christ is the High Priest for His

bride, the Church, men are called to perform priestly duty by representing their families before Him. It's by divine design, not because he must be dominant. The first responsibility of a priest *is to sanctify himself* so he can stand blameless before a holy God!

"Confessing and repenting of one's own sins is a humbling experience for anyone, regardless of gender. When I am beholden to His grace to even stand in His presence, entrusted with a family precious in His sight, my heart is humbled, not lifted up.

"I can't lead those I love forcefully. It's not in me! From what I've seen, those who aggressively assert their authority do so to hide a failure to sanctify themselves in the first place. Before presenting an offering to God, sin must be put away *first*. That kind of pride is sinful!

"Let me share something with you. Erin and I *did* disagree about buying the new house in Missouri. Had she just followed my lead, we wouldn't have done it. I didn't have the faith to do it! With a lifetime of following Christ, my faith still didn't measure up to hers, I'm ashamed to admit.

"The money we have is primarily hers." Erin began to object, but stopped when he looked at her, "I know, honey. I'm just making a point."

He gave her hand a squeeze and she nodded.

"She loved the place. She could have made the deal without me, Carol, but refused to do so. Because she prayed with me, I was inspired and convinced the Lord wanted this for us. Only when we were in agreement did we move forward.

"Thank God I didn't get my way, influenced as it was by fear! Erin was right about the way we should go; however, she didn't insist on it, even so. We were both committed to doing the Lord's will *together*, with no one left behind.

"A house divided against itself cannot stand,"

remember? Christ is able to put our hearts in agreement. I can muster enough faith to believe *that*."

Their girls were in tears, not knowing all this. They weren't alone!

Erin spoke up, her eyes wet, too. "Carol, I was an orphan, so I know how it feels. The idea I can comfort others who have known that feeling is beyond my ability to ignore! To do it without Allen beside me would have been like ripping my heart out! I couldn't. I couldn't take away his fear, either. I had to trust Jesus, to let Him do it. I also had to let Allen see he meant too much to me to do it without his agreement.

"I've broken many men. Machismo doesn't impress me, not at all! This man *does*, day in and day out. The more I get to know him, the more I admire him. There is nothing phony about him, just layer after layer of humanity with a capacity to love I never dreamed humanly possible!

"If I had not met Jesus, I'd worry that another disappointing male would someday be revealed in him, but meeting Him caused me to understand His servant. I see Jesus in him, and I love what I see. If you get a glimpse of your husband in the same light, it will change your marriage like nothing else will!"

Carol gripped Tom's arm with both of hers, a little smile on her face. "There *are* times, when I just... I think I know what you mean, Erin."

The elder woman continued, "I can take charge, bark orders to get people moving when it seems appropriate. Some would call me a natural leader for this ability. It would be tough to run a company if I couldn't! My man says he can't, thinks I'm a better leader than he is. I disagree.

"The righteousness in him sets an example that challenges everyone around him to excellence. He does it unconsciously, not even aware he's doing it! *I can't do that.*

"Everyone here knows he's our leader, but it's not because he means to be. He isn't competitive. Our relationship would be a constant tug-of-war, if he was. I'm competitive enough for both of us!"

Allen had to chuckle. Truer words were never spoken!

She grinned at his amusement. "His knowledge of scripture and God's ways has blessed us, but that's not what causes us to fall in behind him, either. Jesus nailed it when He told me to comfort His *servant*. He serves the Lord with a devotion to us that bonds us to him better than superglue! Jesus said the greatest among us would be the servant of all, you know. My husband exemplifies it!"

Well, that was more attention than he was comfortable with. When applause broke out, it didn't help!

Gui came to the rescue. "It's true we know we can count on Allen, but we'd have to respect him, anyway. We've all been taught to respect our elders!"

With a grin, Allen stuck his tongue out at him, resulting in laughter.

His jaw dropped when Reina chimed in, "Careful, son. You don't want him getting cranky when he starts *yawning* again!"

He shook his head as they laughed. "I'm not anybody's leader. Too much abuse comes with the job!"

"We only tease the ones we love," Dani reminded him. "That's a standard *you* set, remember?"

"You *listened* to what I said? Whatever made you think that was a good idea?"

It cracked everyone up. They were having such a good time no one rushed off. Erin ordered pizza to feed the crowd. Friendships grew as they became better acquainted.

Finally, Conrad called for a moment to ask about something. "Allen, we're expecting Jesus to call us home any day now, right?"

He replied with a nod.

"Okay, I'm wondering if you believe the person who

will become the Antichrist is alive now."

Stunned silence awaited his response.

"Yes, I do. I like how one of my favorite Bible teachers, Chuck Missler, used to field that question. He's gone to be with the Lord now. He would say yes, then point out that if asked fifty years ago, his answer would still be the same.

"His logic went like this: Jesus said no man knows the day nor the hour of his return, right?"

Conrad agreed, along with others.

"Well, 'no man' includes Satan! That being the case, he always had to have someone waiting in the wings to assume the role, just in case.

"Some thought Hitler was the Antichrist in his day. Deluded as he was, he didn't think so. A Satanist named Aleister Crowley visited him shortly after he came to power. After their meeting behind closed doors, someone asked how it went. Hitler replied, "I have met the Antichrist, and I was terrified!" It makes me wonder, what could frighten *him*?

"The spirit who will empower that man is loose in the world, yet restrained by the Spirit of God empowering us until He is taken out of the way. When Jesus calls us to Him in the rapture, that particular manifestation of the Holy Spirit will go with us. Then the lawless one will be revealed, according to II Thessalonians, whom the Lord will consume with the breath of His mouth and the brightness of His coming when He returns to set up His kingdom.

"Until he is revealed, we wouldn't know him if we saw him. It's possible *he* doesn't know the role he will play, just yet. It doesn't matter; all scripture will be fulfilled in its time. Nothing is going to surprise God."

He nodded, but being a kid, he followed up to see what more he could get. "Do you have any idea who it might be?"

"Not exactly," Allen replied. "Most seem to expect a master politician. There are scriptures indicating something else to me. I expect a general, a man of war... who may not be entirely human."

You could have heard a pin drop.

He heaved a sigh. "I don't mind expounding, but are you all sure you want to hear this now? We've already talked about so much that stretches the imagination, and this will tax it further! I don't want to overload anyone."

The younger folks wanted to dive right into it. Others weighed his concern until Ted broke his silence to make a proposal. "Allen, you have a point. The kids have school tomorrow, and we have work, as interesting as all this is."

There were groans of disappointment.

"How about this: can you share a few of those scriptures you're talking about, give us something to chew on until we get together again?"

"I can do that," he smiled. "I don't have chapter and verse references ready off the top of my head, but they're not hard to look up. Consider it optional homework, if anyone is sufficiently interested in it.

"Okay, in Revelation Antichrist is referred to as *the Beast*, not just by God, but by the world as well. They will say, *"Who is like the Beast? And who can make war with Him?"* It implies they have seen him fight so effectively he appears to be impossible to beat! They respect his capabilities on the battlefield, may even fear him.

"This raises a question. Wouldn't calling him *the Beast* risk provoking him to anger? It sounds insulting, or at least disrespectful to my ears, yet he apparently doesn't take offense. Why? Perhaps there is *literally* something of a beast about him, a genetic difference giving him a superhuman advantage over others. If he takes pride in that difference, he might like being called 'The Beast.'

"The Mark of the Beast seems to point that way! Many get caught up in the economic aspects of the prophecy, but it is first and foremost a mark of loyalty to him, the reason whoever takes it will be excluded from Heaven. Whether it involves a subcutaneous chip or not, *something* will be plainly visible to the naked eye, identifying with the Beast himself! It may be partly artificial, but some aspect of it is transformational, similar to a werewolf's bite, though surely less dramatic.

"More, or is that enough for now?" he paused for their response.

"There's *more*?" Win wanted to know, his eyes wide.

"I think you read us right, Allen," Dani breathed. "This is overload, right now."

Conrad grinned, "We can stop. This is stuff my brother will want to hear, too."

Tom shook his head. "We've studied Revelation multiple times, but we never gleaned from it the way you do. Let's get back to it later."

"Fair enough," he returned with a smile. "I'm glad we'll be with the Lord when all this happens!"

The reflection caused everyone to heave a sigh of relief. Visiting turned to lighter matters as some began to say goodnight. The couple reminded them since they planned to fly home the next day, there would be no conference call until Tuesday. The thought of staying in touch seemed to reassure the two new families, making goodbyes easier for them. Allen invited Ted and Hans to call him whenever they liked. He'd be happy to visit, if they wanted. They seemed to appreciate the offer.

It was no surprise when their girls lingered. Carlos and Juanita hung around, though, which he didn't expect. It wasn't long before they expressed what was on their minds.

CHAPTER 8

"**L**aurie brought something up that interests us, especially what you told her," Carlos recalled.
His wife smiled, holding his hand and nodding agreement.

"She asked what reigning with Jesus will be like. You know me; I want to know what to look forward to with Him! You said you might have some insight. Are you up for telling us about it now?"

Laurie's expression brightened, pleased to have the subject revisited.

"If it won't overload us," Emily added quickly.

Dani nodded, glancing her way.

"No, this isn't weighty," he reassured them. "I find it encouraging to think about, actually. The Bible doesn't elaborate very much on the millennial reign of Christ following the Tribulation. Chapters describe the seven years, but the thousand years get little coverage, and it's peppered throughout scripture.

"We will have Christ with us by that time, so we don't need to prepare for it. He will direct us. In our glorified immortal bodies, we'll also have the mind of Christ ourselves. Our thoughts will be as His, so it will be easy to collaborate with Him."

He had the rapt attention of his listeners.

"When you walk with the Lord in fellowship over time, He likes to share tidbits with His disciples of a personal nature. It's like a father delighting in a moment of intimacy with one of his kids. It might be cluing the child in on something he's not yet aware is in store for him, or it might be to give him a puzzle piece toward forming the big picture only the father has envisioned, so far. It seems marvelous, but the best part is realizing you have His personal attention!

"In one of those moments, I had a dream unlike any before or since. I was in a subway car as it traveled down the tracks, alone at one end. A handful of riders were on it at the other end, but they had no idea I was there. I was invisible! They seemed bored, unenthused.

"I would think of a question and instantly know the answer. Where was I? The New York Subway. Where are all the people? There aren't many, anymore. What happened? The Tribulation and Armageddon depopulated the world, so people are rare!"

His audience's eyes were widening by the moment.

"Who rules this world now? I grinned as it came to me Jesus rules in Jerusalem! Could I see Him? Instantly I knew I could reach out to open a window in midair, so we could speak face to face. I could even step *through* the window to be with Him!

"Several things fell into place. He had sent me to maintain order where I was. Though I was on the opposite side of the world from Him, there was a *connection* holding me to Him. I was never alone and never would be again! If I chose to go to Him, He wouldn't be angry that I left my post, just glad to see me. Knowing this, I was satisfied to remain where He placed me.

"Where was my wife? On assignment, just like me. South America came to mind, with an understanding; if I missed her too much, I could open the window to tell Jesus. He would gladly open another window I could step through to be with her. It was like nothing I could ask for would displease Him or disrupt His plans! We were all connected through Him.

"Looking at the few in the subway car with me, I was aware I could make myself visible. Had I done so, they would not have been afraid, just might have wondered why I was there. They would recognize me as one of those reigning with Christ. I could stop sin in progress, judge and pass sentence on the spot! However, with nothing like that happening, my appearance would just arouse mild curiosity.

"I elected not to disturb them. Like a swimmer underwater, it felt like I swung my arms down to propel myself toward the surface, then I was floating above the train, watching it pass beneath me. I had *immense* power! If the train derailed, I could easily hold it to the tracks to prevent disaster. Preparing to go above ground, I thrust down again... and woke up."

Laurie's eyes were like saucers. "You think it will be like your dream?"

"I honestly don't know, sweetie. Scripture doesn't give that much detail. However, what little I saw *does fit* with what the Bible says. We will judge the nations, Paul said. We will reign with Christ. A time is prophesied when a man will be rarer than the gold of Ophir! This word has yet to be fulfilled, but seemed to be the case in the dream.

"I actually saw precious little of the world around me, and I never saw myself at all, but there was something very different about me. Had I appeared to those present, they would have known I represented Christ on sight, but it didn't occur to me to wonder how. The Bible says we will know as we are known. God knows everything about us, even the number of hairs on our heads... and anything I wanted to know, I did!

"I think I was given a glimpse of what it will be like for us. There's no way to tell for sure until the time comes. Whether it's like that or not, I don't believe it's possible for us to be disappointed with what He reveals."

"You want to know what *I* think?" Erin had a small smile on her face.

"*Always*, Genie," he replied, as the rest nodded.

"When I saw Jesus, He radiated light. His appearance was so bright, I couldn't see Him clearly! I think those on the train would have known you were His because you would *shine* like He does! God is our Father, but you said He is called the Father of Lights, remember?"

"Whoa!" came from several mouths as they all grinned. It sounded *right*! The insight thrilled them.

"Our whole family should hear this, Allen," Carlos pointed out.

Juanita nodded, "It's uplifting, something to look forward to!"

They visited until Stef returned, then separated reluctantly. Stef assured them they would see the couple again in two months, perhaps sooner. When asked where she got that idea, she shrugged, smiled and chalked it up to intuition. Nothing more definite was forthcoming.

It sounded mysterious, but Erin pointed out Stef's intuition was usually reliable, so the rest were encouraged as they left. The four remaining, with Emily, visited some more before calling it a night. Their flight wasn't scheduled early, so they could afford to stay up. Stef told Emily she hoped to see her on future visits. The Ukrainian was pleased, but said it would depend on her schedule, once she had her new life sorted out. Stef said she understood.

Allen told their hostess, "You'll have your bedroom back tomorrow! You must be looking forward to it."

She chuckled, "Yeah, it'll be nice, but you guys' visit more than made up for the minor inconvenience of sleeping in the bunk room. When my best friends are near, I sleep better than usual. I can't explain it. Having you here feels right. I'm gonna miss you."

He invited her to lean on Laurie, Dani and Pam more in their absence, saying they wouldn't mind. She felt it would be an unfair imposition on employees. It might be, he agreed, but we're also *family*. That changes things!

The smile on her face brightened when they reminded her of the contribution she was making by training Fran and Denise to protect themselves. They all appreciated it! Besides, she was supportive of Laurie and Dani in the challenges they faced with their parents. Friendship works best when there is give and take both ways.

"You know if you ever need us, one call will bring us running," Erin stated.

"Yeah, I know," Stef admitted, "but I wouldn't do that to you. If I can't handle my own problems by now, I'll never be able to."

It occurred to him *that* independence was what kept her from receiving God's grace in Christ Jesus!

He turned to Erin, "Maybe it's for the best. She is just so *needy*!"

Erin and Emily burst out laughing, while Stef's jaw dropped open. A slow smile turned to laughter as his words were absorbed.

"Would I be pushing my luck to quote a bit of wisdom to you?" he asked Stef.

"From the Bible?" she wanted to know, still chuckling.

"No, this comes from a well-known Italian philosopher named Dean Martin. You've probably heard of him."

She grinned.

"His theme song stated "Everybody needs somebody, sometimes." If it ever becomes true in your case, maybe we can be *somebody* for you, okay?"

"Okay, when you put it that way," she laughed again.

CHAPTER 9

The following day, the nearer they got to home, the more excited Emily became. It was fun to watch! Her eyes bugged out when they pulled in the driveway. "I'm going to live *here*?"

Erin chuckled, "We've got room, so you might as well."

Emily's grin was so wide her face glowed. Heidi came out to greet them with hugs. She welcomed the Gypsy girl enthusiastically and told her it was going to be *so much fun* having her there! Helping gather their luggage, she said Ruth was waiting inside. When they walked in, Ruth stood to embrace them all.

That did it! Tears came unbidden down Emily's cheeks. She apologized.

Ruth laughed, a few tears of her own springing forth. "Don't worry about it, honey. You're home now. You can call me Ruth or Grandma, whatever you're more comfortable with."

Allen laughed, "Laurie is already calling you

Grandma, Mom."

She chuckled, "There's nothing wrong with that. I can hardly wait to meet her and Danielle, too!"

Ruth and Heidi were pleased to show Emily her room. In the week they had learned she was coming, they dressed it up to welcome her. Heidi selected the room across the hall from her own. They collaborated to lightly adorn the bare walls and decorate, furnishing frilled curtains of red and white, colors Emily was known to favor. She was thrilled! They told her they only meant for it to be welcoming. She could personalize it to her own satisfaction, could change it any way she wanted.

Grinning, she opened her handbag, pulled out her Bible and placed it on the nightstand, then announced, "Done!"

All laughed as she flopped on the bed, covered with a bedspread and pillow cases matching the curtains.

"I love it, just like it is! I want pictures of all of you for the walls in time, but for now, it's perfect!"

They gave her a tour of the house before dinner. She was delighted with the layout, particularly the observatory. She asked if they could read together there. Allen agreed, explaining to the others what the two of them discussed about building her reading skills and how he had sort of volunteered their help.

They were enthusiastic! Ruth said *this* was something she could do!

She offered to give them rent right away, promising to find work as soon as possible. Erin told her rent would wait until she had income. The job search could start the following week. She was urged to settle in and get comfortable during her first week home.

Heidi was thrilled to have a buddy to hang with and gladly showed her around town. Only a few days passed until Emily followed Heidi home in a car she picked out. She proudly showed it off, a pretty VW bug. Allen laughed at first, but when she took them for a joyride and let him drive, his perspective changed. It was fun to drive, downright peppy! Congratulating her, he apologized for laughing, to her amusement. He said as long as she was happy with it, that's all that matters, anyway.

The conference calls kept everyone connected, not only on a personal level, but in the exploration of God's Word. Truly amazing things are depicted on its pages! The Spirit of Truth opened the contents so those new to it were hooked, while those acquainted with it were refreshed, finding new gems each time.

Lively discussions often ensued. When testimonies tied in with what they were studying, the present linked with the past to show how Christ still worked in their midst.

An example came forth during the study of Acts chapter eight. Philip the evangelist (a deacon, not one of the twelve apostles) was led by the Holy Spirit into the desert to testify to an Ethiopian official returning home from Jerusalem. The man received Christ on hearing Philip's presentation and asked to be baptized. Upon doing so, Philip vanished, reappearing in a town to the north. He preached his way home from there!

It was mind-blowing for those who hadn't heard it before! The lone Biblical instance of teleportation made a hot topic. Questions came at Allen rapid-fire, most beyond his ability to answer definitively. He told them while he didn't have all the answers, he'd give them the best he had. The line went quiet in response.

"I can't say why the Lord chose to supernaturally move his servant on this occasion. It had to be a sign to the caravan, probably even to Philip himself. Surely, none of them ever forgot it! When God does something we can't do, it's not easily forgotten. I wonder if Philip ever learned why the Lord did it. Scripture doesn't say.

"Like Nebuchadnezzar's account in Daniel, there is nothing else in the Bible like it. Since the scripture is perfect, there has to be a reason it was included for us."

He recalled aloud that perhaps what the proud Babylonian king experienced wasn't unique, after all. Similarly proud and *dangerous* beings the general population is not fully aware of may also be held at bay until the time of lawlessness arrives.

"However, what happened to Philip *wasn't* unique. I say that with certainty, because the same kind of thing happened to me, a long time ago."

Expressions of surprise resulted at his declaration, but no one interrupted.

"In the winter of 1992-93, my first wife and I lived in Carlsbad, New Mexico. Anthony was born in mid-'93; we knew nothing of him yet, since we only received two months' notice to initiate his adoption before he was born. We went for a drive near the lake, in an area we were not familiar with, for an outing.

"Carlsbad's main highway runs north and south through town. The lake parallels it on the northeast side. At the lake's south tip, a four-lane highway starts off eastward, toward a town called Hobbs. The Hobbs highway never downsizes; it's four lanes all the way. We turned north off of it to follow the lake, eventually turning eastward, just exploring. I have a strong sense of direction and no fear of getting lost, so we kept going until the light began to fade.

"I turned us south at that point, knowing we'd have to approach the Hobbs highway eventually from the north. A right turn would then take us back into town. There is no other four-lane highway in the area, nothing that might confuse us. We went south for a long time as darkness fell, well out of town into the boonies.

"We didn't have GPS or a cell phone then," he pointed out, hearing chuckles. "Instead of finding the highway, we were forced to turn east again at one point. Rather than reverse course, I followed the road until it curved north and kept going. Nothing was out there, not even an occasional house. It was opposite of the way I wanted to go. I was getting worried when we came up to a four-lane highway!"

"We sat there for a couple of minutes. I wondered if my sense of direction had completely failed me. She wanted me to go, but I told her I wasn't sure which way. A faint glow of lights rose over the hills to the left, a hint the city was that way. It meant we approached the highway from the south.

"She was okay with this conclusion. I wasn't! We would've had to *cross the highway* at some point to be where we were. She admitted we never crossed a four-lane highway while we were wandering.

"I decided to turn right, according to my common sense. A few miles down the highway was a sign marking the miles remaining to reach Hobbs. We turned around, re-entering Carlsbad about 15 minutes later. *It was impossible!* Somehow, we traveled from a point northeast of the city to south of the highway without crossing it. My sense of direction was right the whole time, but at some point, the Lord *relocated* us.

"It was years later before I received anything other than peace from Him about it. She never seemed bugged over it, just put it behind her. It stuck with me, though. God never does anything without a reason. If He was making a point, it had to be for us. No one else even knew what happened!"

"I took a page out of your book, Dani, persevering until He finally gave me something."

She chuckled.

"This is the response I received, years later: *The way you are going is no indication of where you will end up. I will place you where I want you at the appointed time.* The idea that He used such a mighty deed to make His point, to provide such an unforgettable sign, blew me away!"

"It turned out to be true, didn't it?" Fran observed.

"Yeah, it did, in a bigger way than I ever dreamed. I

have a new partner, a new and growing family... and I'm useful to you all. I felt like I was pretty much just a meal ticket before, and not a very reliable one."

"It sounds like you were your own worst critic, Allen," Hans pointed out.

"I always have been, truthfully," he confessed.

Erin shook her head, taking his hand in both of hers comfortingly.

"I don't like the way you're talking about my dad, so stop it!" Laurie rebuked him sternly.

"I can't help how I *used to feel*, honey. I don't feel like that anymore! How can I? Philip had four daughters who prophesied, which we'll read later. In a way, I'm like him, and not just because of a similar experience. I also have four precious young ladies I think of as my girls. I couldn't love you more than I already do, you know?"

The two present laid reassuring hands on him and grinned.

After a moment, Dani acknowledged, "We know."

Laurie sniffled wordlessly.

"You've also got brothers and sisters," Carol stated.

"And a niece," Alissa broke in with a giggle.

"Some nephews, too," Eli inserted.

"That's right! And we all expect Christmas presents!" Erik announced to laughter.

"Erik!" his mother reprimanded him.

"That's exactly what I would have said, at his age," Guillermo declared. "He's gonna do us proud, Allen!"

The older man agreed with a smile..

CHAPTER 10

Conrad had been thinking. "I have a question. Satan likes to counterfeit what God does, you know? Is it possible this account is in scripture to keep us from being deceived? If a time comes when Satan does something like this, we'll understand God did it first. The devil never does anything original, we've been taught, but without this passage, teleporting would seem original."

Someone said, "Oh, wow!"

Allen replied, "Conrad, I think you're onto something. It may be the chief reason this account exists! I hadn't thought of it, but it makes sense. Do you remember what we talked about before, when we discussed Bigfoot?"

He did. So did everyone else, the response indicated.

"I believe in being driven away from us, the unclean offspring of angelic rebellion has been granted some fringe access to the spiritual realm. The Watchers permitted this to keep them from being cornered, to prevent otherwise inevitable confrontations. Those beings hate us, fleeing reluctantly. They were once the kings of the Earth, would slaughter people gladly to regain their former dominion!

"When they step into the spiritual realm, earthly distance is irrelevant. They can step back into this world a few feet away from their starting point, or hundreds of miles distant. From our perspective, that's teleporting! It would make it impossible to corner them, taking away any excuse they might invent to force a confrontation where they could justify defending themselves to our harm.

"Who is like the Beast? And who can make war with him?" People will wonder in the time of lawlessness to come, known as the Tribulation. It seems the Antichrist will have some decisive advantage making it humanly impossible to overcome him. If he weaponizes teleportation, that might do it! How could you fight an enemy who can appear behind you without notice? You wouldn't even see him coming!"

"Technology would be useless against that," Pam said quietly. "Surgical strikes by a handful of soldiers could overwhelm any nation's defenses overnight, even this one!"

Nodding agreement, Allen continued, "Ten kings will rule the world when he appears. He will overthrow three in his rise to power. After Jesus comes for His Bride and evacuates the Church, the world will hunker down in fear, probably expecting an alien invasion! Consolidation of power to unite against a common enemy would sound like a smart move, but the invasion comes from the shadows, not space."

"I remember Ronald Reagan saying nothing would unite the world quicker than an alien threat," Reina mused. "No wonder the devil keeps deceiving people with UFOs! People who deny the rapture will have to blame aliens. Nothing else will make sense!"

"There's the lie to set the stage for the Antichrist!" Ted made the connection. "If he waves his hand to make the UFOs go away, it will seem as though he saved the world single-handedly!"

Allen responded, *"... God will send them strong delusion, that they should believe a lie, because they would not receive the love of the truth, that they might be saved."* That's in II Thessalonians. When millions vanish in an instant heeding our Lord's summons, *billions* will panic, seeking answers.

"Any rejecting the truth will need a whopper of a lie to take its place! UFOs are the only reasonable explanation, it seems to me. Ted's right! Someone who apparently can make them go away would seem like the messiah to a world cringing in fear!"

"Wouldn't he want to flaunt how he can command them, rather than send them away?" Erin put in. "He'd seem even more powerful, if he co-opted them."

"He might, at first. If they are perceived as a threat by the world, though, permitting them to remain would garner mistrust in the masses. He wants the world's loyalty! His mark is officially a sign of loyalty.

"UFOs are a deception, evil angels projecting images of ships or lights. When Michael and his troops cast those rebellious angels down to Earth, denying them the skies thereafter, Antichrist's power would take a big blow by affiliation. He'd be better off holding power independently, rallying mortals to Armageddon."

Tom pointed out, "That's another deception, since his power comes from Satan!"

"You're right, but at least he doesn't seem to command Satan. I doubt the Devil's ego would be pleased to endure that charade for long! Pride led to his fall, remember?"

Liz spoke, "Good point! He'd rather be worshipped, like God."

Their conference call came to an end shortly thereafter.

Bart Palombo was less than impressed with Springfield, Missouri. He was used to the finer things in life, like his tower apartment overlooking the coast of Lake

Michigan in Chicago. Travel was a necessary evil in his line of work, though. At least this assignment wasn't taking him too far afield, but something in the air was giving him fits with his allergies! Sinus drainage was making him miserable.

He drove the distance. The kind of equipment his work required was... specialized... in a way he'd rather not explain to strangers. His car eliminated any such need. Everything had its place customized within. It would take a determined search to uncover anything incriminating. Bart was careful in such matters. It made him successful in a field that naturally weeded out the careless in short order.

He arrived in the early evening. He shouldn't have been tired, but allergies had him exhausted. After stopping to get medication and eat, he checked into a motel, intent on getting some rest. Clear eyes would keep his job simple, not to mention he couldn't afford uncontrolled sneezing! *That* could be the end of him!

CHAPTER 11

Danielle had a friend with her for most visits with her father, but there were occasions when she went alone. He seemed to be withdrawing into himself; it was hard to watch. On one such visit, when it seemed he took no notice of her, she began telling him how she gave her life to Jesus. She poured out how His forgiveness revolutionized her life and lifted the burdens of sin and depression to fill her heart with joy.

He had been staring ahead vacantly, but his head turned toward her. Speaking softly, he told her, "Your mother saw Him, you know."

Her breath caught momentarily, "She did?"

He nodded, "At the end, through the pain, she said she saw Him reaching out to her. She cried and asked forgiveness, apologizing to Him by name. Her face lit up with joy as she reached out, then she was gone. I always wondered afterward if it was real, or just the pain and medication talking."

Tears ran down her cheeks. Her mom was in Heaven!

She had no idea, before this.

"I want... I want to be with her again, my Dani girl." He called her that growing up; she hadn't heard it in years. "If Jesus has her, will He have me, too?"

Laughing and crying at the same time, she led her dad to Christ in his precious moment of clarity. He thanked her and Jesus profusely. The tension constantly radiating from his posture drained away noticeably, replaced with a huge smile. He was finally at peace.

"I crumbled when she passed. It wasn't right to you kids, but she was my world! I missed her *too* much. You stepped into her shoes and raised your brother when I couldn't... get it together. It wasn't fair to either of you. Can you forgive me?"

"Already done, Dad," she assured him, her hand on his arm.

"No, it's not, not completely," he disagreed, giving her a wry smile. "If it was totally done, you wouldn't feel the need to beat up boys!"

She burst out laughing in surprise. He laughed, too. "It's just a way to make a living, Dad. It's not..."

His head was shaking, "You're only fooling yourself, sweetheart. You couldn't help losing your mother, but it made you angry when you lost me, too. Your anger internalized as depression, while expressing itself as aggression toward men, like me! Jesus will show you, if you ask Him. I failed you, but the truth will set you free."

He looked out the window. "My thoughts... are like birds flying away. I can't help it. Jesus brought me to myself today, so you could lead me to Him and I could help you, just a little bit. I hope I did. Let me go, honey. Staying with this body of mine is too much for you. Wherever my thoughts fly, Jesus is with me now, so I'll be okay."

His voice was growing distant as he spoke; she knew she was losing him. It caused her to hang on every coherent word he uttered.

"Tell your brother... what Jesus did for all of us. Let the new family He gave you... love you like He does... like I do..."

He was gone again. Unintelligible muttering accompanied the vacant stare out the window. The Lord's presence covered her like a cloak, comforting her in spite of her tears. She had been relieved of her vigil; he had willingly put himself in Christ's care. It was just as well, since her ability to reach him had been slipping away.

She stood, hugged him without receiving a response, and said aloud, "Thank you, Jesus. I'm leaving him in Your hands, then. 'Bye, for now, Dad. I love you, too." Peace was her companion as she left.

Laurie cried when Dani told her what happened, tender-hearted as ever. She reassured the younger woman she'd stay until Laurie's business in L.A. was finished, so they could leave for Missouri together. It earned her a huge hug in gratitude. She did say she planned to take vacation time to go visit her brother, but would return afterward.

"Do you think your dad was right?" Laurie inquired. "Did you become a wrestler out of anger at him? The reason I'm asking is it makes me wonder if my anger at my mother influenced my choice, too."

Dani thought a moment before responding. "I honestly don't know. He seemed so sure... I'm gonna have to give it some thought. I do enjoy the challenge. It's fun to take a man's chauvinistic pride and wring it out! It doesn't get weird for me until I come close to losing. Then it's like I get angry at myself, or so I thought. I become determined not to surrender. I wonder if it's the same for Pam? Maybe I'll ask her.

"Jesus changed my heart, so even if it started that way for me, it's not the same now. I don't think anger motivated your choice, though. Even when you left home, it was more out of hurt than anger, in my opinion. He guided you here because you needed love, and I needed *you!*"

Laurie responded with a happy grin.

"You wrestle because you enjoy the physicality and the opportunity to excel. You love to compete. If your mother hadn't ruined gymnastics for you, it would have been a natural fit. I think you get a bigger kick out of making men cave than I do!"

Chuckling, Laurie nodded.

"Whatever the case, the Lord led us here, no question."

"That's true," Laurie agreed. "Erin wasn't as expressive in those days before meeting Dad, but we both knew she cared about us, in her own way. Who knew God would bring a special man into her life, then change us so completely, binding us all together in the process?"

Dani shook her head, "No one could have known what He planned, sis. It's better than anything we could have dreamed up!"

CHAPTER 12

E mily started a new job working at a bowling alley during her third week in Springfield. Even though it didn't sound exciting, her joy reminded them of Laurie. Her reading was already showing improvement in this short period. When she said Gypsies are social people, she wasn't kidding! She was nearly always with one or more of them, even if they were just sitting quietly. It thrilled her, no longer being alone.

In the same week, Heidi shared a dream or perhaps a vision; she wasn't sure which. Viewing the house from the front, she saw a man in glowing white robes standing before it like a sentry. He was thirty feet tall and held an unsheathed sword, ready for battle! She understood he was an angel standing guard over the household. *No one* would get past him to do them harm! They smiled at the thought.

The next day, a knock came at the door. A Springfield Police officer was there with a man and woman dressed in suits, asking to speak with Heidi. They invited them in, while Emily went to get Heidi from Ruth's room. Everyone came to see what was up. Heidi asked if it was okay. All three visitors agreed it was.

The local policeman introduced himself as Brian Henstead, then introduced Agents Cooper and Smythe of the FBI. That raised eyebrows! He said they were there in the course of an investigation they would explain, stating plainly Heidi was in no way implicated. Ruth suggested everyone settle at the dining room table.

He began to relate a strange tale. Four days earlier, Springfield Police responded to a traffic accident. A man lost control of his car to jump a curb, rolling down a small embankment to land upside down. Not wearing a seatbelt, he was killed instantly, his head crushed. Noting allergy medications were present, investigators postulated he lost control when he spilled hot coffee on himself, possibly when he sneezed!

Though it was a freak accident, what they found in the wreckage gave them pause. He was carrying a cherrywood-handled pistol covered with tiny notches. A hidden compartment in the trunk broke open in the rollover, releasing a custom metal case. Within was a high-powered rifle, a scope and silencers for both guns. This pointed toward the man being an assassin, so federal authorities were contacted.

He deferred to his companions. Agent Smythe related how ballistics from the two guns were cross-referenced with cold case files. The search linked them to more than twenty unsolved murders so far, and the number was still rising! It was a coup for law enforcement, since the man never brought suspicion on himself. He was generically listed in Chicago as an independent 'investment consultant' reporting a moderate income to the IRS. His true occupation was completely camouflaged, until his demise!

Agent Cooper explained their presence. It took some time to gain access to his phone, and when they did, the results were disappointing. No incriminating records were found, neither calls nor transactions. They believed he had a database on the dark web and were looking for it. A *lot* of cash had been found in a safe in his apartment, but it couldn't be traced to those who hired him.

What they did find was Heidi's name and picture. Given the man's vocation, they believed he may have targeted her, the reason he was in Springfield. Was there anyone who might have paid to have her killed?

The color drained from her face.

Ruth was beside her. She touched her arm to get her attention. "The Lord knew about this, honey. It's *why* He showed you the angel."

The policeman tilted his head quizzically. The Feds listened intently without reaction.

Erin added, "The man is dead. He can't hurt you now!"

Agent Smythe reinforced their reassurance. "We didn't mean to scare you. We want to put away everyone who hired him, as many as we can find. If we can get whoever wants you dead, you'll be safer for it! We certainly don't want you to get hurt. Let us help you."

She pursed her lips.

"It's my fault," Allen spoke up. "On a visit to California, Erin and I met Heidi. I told her about Jesus Christ, which resulted in leading her to put her faith in Him. Her mother took it personally! She leads a coven of witches. Her daughter receiving Christ was viewed as an embarrassment. Her death has been called for ever since!"

"She came to live with us to get clear of all that," Erin added.

"Your own mother wants you dead?" Officer Henstead was flabbergasted.

Heidi nodded.

Agent Cooper sat back and glanced at Agent Smythe. "Well, it's not the strangest thing I've ever heard, but it makes the top ten. Does she have the money to put a contract out on you?"

They all looked at Heidi.

She nodded emphatically, "Big time. She used to brag about how close she was to having her first billion, probably has it now. She's behind this, but you'll never prove it, no matter what you do. She's extremely careful not to incriminate herself!"

Agent Smythe gave her a smile, "You let us worry about that. We're very good at what we do. If we had this kind of heads-up on the dead assassin, we would have shut him down a long time ago!"

She apparently thought Heidi would be relieved by her words, but the tall redhead caught her off-guard with a plea.

"I grew up with her, so I know what she's capable of. Please don't put any agents in harm's way trying to get evidence on her! *She'll know.* Your people will get hurt, maybe killed. It's not worth it!"

They stood to leave, promising to be careful. Allen's impression was they considered her overwrought, not recognizing her wisdom for what it was. The policeman handed her his card. She thanked him by name.

He told her to call him Brian. "If you ever need anything, just call. You have a friend on the Force now!"

The whole family appreciated it!

CHAPTER 13

Brian called Heidi a couple of days later, asking if it would be alright to pay a visit while off-duty. He'd like to ask some questions, but nothing official. The FBI was long gone. They set up a time.

When he arrived, he presented her with a dozen red roses! The rest grinned as they both blushed. He said he felt bad the first visit evoked so much fear and hoped to make it up to her. Shaking her head, she said he was just doing his job and there was no harm done. They settled in the living room this time.

Out of uniform, Allen took notice of his appearance. He was tall, though it looked like Heidi had an inch on him, rangy and well-built. Handsome, too, blond-haired with a trimmed mustache. He guessed his age at thirty or so. The ladies had discussed his good looks after the first visit, so Allen was more attentive. He concluded they had a point!

Ruth's comment about Heidi seeing an angel had him curious. He explained he identified as a Christian and had attended a huge Assembly of God church in the area for years. On official business, he couldn't pursue the subject in the agents' presence, but he was *very* interested. The church he attended was considered progressive, yet in years of attendance, nothing overtly supernatural had happened to him.

Heidi related her vision. His jaw dropped. Ruth told him it was given to her in advance, letting her know the Lord was seeing to her safety. Nothing could escape His sight!

Allen added in his opinion, the accident that slew her would-be assassin was no accident. God saw the threat and simply took him out! It pleased Him to do so in such a way that he was revealed at last for what he was, a hired killer.

Brian chewed it over, shaking his head. "It makes sense. The Good Shepherd protects his flock, even when we don't see danger coming. The thought makes me feel better! I was worried how I - *we* could keep you safe in the face of unidentified threats like the one the hit man posed."

"You're a good man, Officer Henstead," Allen noted, "especially when your concern takes you half a mile outside your jurisdiction on behalf of a young lady who has become dear to us."

"Well… Truthfully, my interest goes beyond duty," he admitted bashfully. "Heidi is about the most beautiful woman I've ever laid eyes on. I was hoping you might consider going out with me?" The request was aimed at her.

Emily giggled.

Heidi smiled, "That might be arranged. Since you're here, let's all get better acquainted for now, then get back to the idea in a bit. Fair enough?"

A big smile indicated it was. He told them about growing up in a small town in southern Illinois, the middle child of three. A cop was all he ever wanted to be. Their neighborhood was patrolled by a kind sergeant everyone knew and trusted implicitly. His willingness to help the people he served inspired Brian to follow his example. Once he finished training, he accepted a position in Springfield six years ago.

"So your mother is a *witch*? Something tells me your story is going to make mine sound boring," he chuckled.

Heidi grimaced, "This is why I wanted to keep my new family around me during our visit." She appraised them gratefully. "I'm not sure I'd believe the story you're about to hear, if I were sitting in your place, hearing it for the first time. I promise, it's all true!"

"I was a witch, too. It's all I knew, being raised by one, surrounded by her coven! A demon I welcomed at age 16 was my closest companion, until this man I adopted as my dad cast him out a few months ago," she gestured toward Allen.

Brian's eyes were getting wider by the moment!

"What he told you before was true. However, our meeting *wasn't* peaceful. Jesus did what Jesus always does. He turned a disaster into a testimony, saving my soul in the process!"

She turned to them, "Mom, Dad, would you tell him what God did for you, leading into my testimony? It won't be complete unless you set the background. I didn't know love until *you* showed it to me."

They did. Allen's background wasn't so different from his, though the end of his long first marriage drew an expression of sympathy. He had difficulty processing Erin's, though! He almost interrupted to question her claim, stopping himself with a distinct effort.

She paused, asking if he believed her. To his credit, he said he was trying. Putting his questions on the back burner, he asked her to continue and forgive his surprise at her... vocation. Amused, she nodded before going forward.

He was absorbed as Erin and Allen shared how God brought about their union and her salvation, so no further interruptions took place. One lone tear streaked his cheek when she described the encounter with Jesus at her salvation. All who love Him long to see His face!

Allen was the primary narrator for his near-death encounter. It brought up emotions making it tough for the ladies to describe. The policeman's head shook slightly as he took it in, Erin, Heidi and even Emily sharing perspectives of the experience. Ruth sat in tears, thanking God under her breath.

The Lord's presence was unmistakable.

When the tale was told, he said, "Whew! I live for Jesus, but not like this! I had no idea stuff like this still happened. It doesn't, in my church."

"Christ shines brightest in broken vessels, Brian," Allen stated quietly. "If we're not trying to present ourselves as better than we are, His grace prevails so His love shines through us. People respond, if anything can move them at all."

"It's what moved me, when I reached the end of myself," Heidi pointed out. "My Enemy became my Deliverer and Savior when I was betrayed. My victim had compassion on me, forgave me to become the dad I never had! Grace just keeps coming, too. I nearly made Erin a widow, yet now she is my mom, loving me like it never happened! I have a grandma and sisters who care about me and fill my heart to the point of bursting! I don't need to pursue power anymore, *because I belong!*"

Allen laughed. "Do you get the impression she feels strongly about this?"

She cracked up, and so did everyone else.

"Yeah, but I can see why," the policeman chuckled. "I think the man she marries better plan to have all of you in his life, too, because I don't think he'll succeed in taking her away from you!"

There was more laughter.

Heidi shook her head vehemently, "Nuh-uh. I belong here, like I said. When they said I could live with them, I told them they'd never be rid of me, and I meant it! If my man thinks differently, a few minutes on the mats in the basement will help him see things my way!"

Emily flinched, "Ooo!"

"Then you ladies *are* wrestlers," he stated more than asked.

All three nodded.

"Having heard all you said, it doesn't seem so incredible now, compared to the rest." He looked uncomfortable.

"Don't worry, I won't hurt you," Heidi grinned.

Allen laid his hand on Erin's knee. She covered it with hers, smiling. "This woman has been reckoned as one of the top ten best in the world today. She's the toughest person I've ever met, easily more than I can handle. Believe me, I know! My own Wonder Woman, but I couldn't ask for a better partner. I can't win against her, yet I can't lose with her!"

The girls were grinning, his wife beaming at the acknowledgement.

His voice went husky. "Brian, God knew what He was doing when He brought her to me. She poses no threat to me. She has become my champion. No human being is more supportive of me, or more careful. Jesus instructed her to comfort me. Her faithfulness will receive His commendation someday! I thank Him constantly for how He blessed me with her."

Her eyes were watering.

"Even when I'm tapping out in one of her submission holds," he added, receiving a sudden burst of laughter.

"Well, this conversation has turned awkward," the policeman observed to chuckles. "Can we talk about something else?"

He learned of their conference call fellowships by asking where they attended church. It bothered him. He referenced the scripture about not forsaking the assembling of brethren together. They looked it up in scripture. In context, it refers to withdrawal as a consequence of being offended. If the offense comes from a person, they agreed forgiveness should prevent alienation. If the offense is toward God's Word, it is an improper response, rather than submission to God.

However, if a church holds to error, refusing reproof, believers are *called* to separate themselves. To remain is to risk being led astray. No one is immune to deception. Ruth had returned to her room to lie down, so all present were surprised when Allen revealed he used to attend the church Brian frequented.

He withdrew when they refused to help with a sudden financial need, unless control of all family resources and income was placed in their hands in a written contract. His protest that the requirement was unbiblical fell on deaf ears, and attempts to speak to the pastor were blocked. He realized any love they might have for brethren was stunted by a love of money.

"I'll never go back," Allen told him.

"What was the need?" Erin inquired.

"Anthony DKA'd and was hospitalized. That's when we learned he had juvenile diabetes. The hospital would bill us, but it was projected to take 45 days to process an application for assistance to get his insulin. We asked the church to help buy the first batch, approximately $600, in the interim. The fact he was a kid did not move them at all!

"God brought us through with samples the doctor managed to gather, also getting our application approved nearly 20 days early. The church cheated itself out of a blessing. In the book of Revelation, the church at Ephesus was doing all the right things, but they left their first love. Jesus warned they would lose their place before Him if they didn't repent!"

"If you've done it unto the least of these my brethren, you've done it unto Me," Erin quoted.

"Could they maybe not have had the money?" Emily checked.

His eyes narrowed, Brian snorted, "No way! You haven't seen this place. They *have* money and have proudly admitted several times that finances are not an issue. I never witnessed anything like this because I never needed their help, but *that* excuse doesn't hold water!"

Allen concurred. "Yeah. While we were there, they supplied a struggling seminary student's family with a brand new minivan, filming its presentation so the congregation could feel they were a part of it. It took more than $20,000 to do it. I didn't question their decision -- it's not my place. I was glad the family was blessed. Still, no lives were at stake. My son's *was*. I still praise God that when they said no, He said yes and amen!"

The conversation turned to other things. When their guest left, Heidi walked out with him. They spoke on the porch briefly. When she returned, Emily asked if she had a date planned. A coy smile with a nod indicated she did.

CHAPTER 14

Nearly a week later, Allen received a call from Guillermo. He was excited! The older man's suggestion had moved him to present his honey glaze to a local honey producer. A test was arranged with their 'hive managers' that absolutely blew them away! They planned to mass-produce his recipe, with assurances he would earn millions.

"I'm gonna be the first millionaire in my family!" he exulted. "Allen, they said honeybee populations have been dwindling in recent years, but my glaze might bring them together to help them repopulate!"

"Naturalists are gonna love you, brother," he chuckled. "I bet bakers will create a demand for it, too, so grocery stores will want to stock it. Just make sure there's a warning on the label, so you don't get sued!"

"I hear you! It's only a matter of time before somebody careless takes it outside and gets stung. Allen, I owe you *so* much! I am free of demons and shame, and now God is setting me up for life... I have no words to express my gratitude!" His voice cracked as he finished.

"Gui, it wasn't me. I can't do anything, apart from Christ. I'm just the tool He used. *Let Him receive all the glory!*

"By the way, at some point, the devil will claim the glaze recipe was his idea, and try to say you owe him. Don't you believe it! His motive was entirely malicious! Already covered with shame, ruining your brother's wedding would have made you want to crawl into a hole and pull a rock over your head! Rebuke him in Jesus' name when he comes around with his lies!"

There was a pause. "You… It's already been popping into my head, Allen, confusing me whether this blessing really came from God. Man, I needed to hear that! Will you pray with me?"

They did.

"You're making me proud, brother," Allen told him afterward. "I believe God showed me the generosity of your heart, how you're gonna make me even more proud. Every selfless act you do is going to fill you with so much joy, it will propel you to another such act, then another. It's like you are being anointed as His version of Santa Claus, honoring Christ all the time. He is giving you wealth, because He knows He can trust you with it."

"Wow! Thank You, Jesus. Let me know if there's ever anything I can do for you, okay?"

"Well, there's one thing, if you don't mind my asking. Erin will want to know, when she hears we spoke. How did it go with Denise? Are you dating?"

He giggled as though caught in mischief. "The answer is yes. You can tell her. My pancake waitress is *awesome*, Allen! I've never dated anyone I respect as much or care so much about what she thinks of me. I think I'm falling for her! Please don't pass it around."

"Got it! Gui's about to be a millionaire, and that's news. Gui may be in love, but that's a secret."

"Perfect! You can tell anyone you want that I love all of you, though. That's no secret!"

"We love you, too, buddy. Stay in touch!"

Erin learned a new trick: how to upgrade conference calls to make them video conferences. It was a hoot, getting to see folks while talking with them. A couple of days later, someone discovered how to use the new connection to get the best of them.

As the call got started, Pam announced angrily, "We have had it!"

Win was uncharacteristically stern, "That's right! We're not going to put up with it anymore!"

Dead silence answered them. Finally Erin asked, "What's wrong?"

Pam declared, "We have decided we just can't go on this way…"

"So we're getting married!" Win completed her statement.

Both broke into huge grins and she held up the engagement ring she wore. Laughter with shrieks of delight answered their declaration. Congratulations preceded news the wedding was scheduled three weeks ahead. While they intended it to be modest and uncomplicated, they begged everyone to attend. Emily had to work, also saying she didn't want to leave Heidi alone if there was trouble. Erin and Allen made plans to go, though, both young ladies insisting on it.

Stefanie called them this time, volunteering her room. Allen felt bad about the imposition, but she dissembled, admitting she liked having them close when they came to town. She reminded them how she predicted they'd be back in two months or less. Her accuracy was a bit uncanny!

Erin chided him after the call. "Haven't you learned there's no point in questioning my partner? She prides herself on her strength, love. Her will is even stronger than her body!"

He grimaced. "I'm not sure that's a good thing, Genie. I wish she wouldn't rebuff the Lord's grace."

"I agree, since there's no salvation apart from Him. She can't stop being who she is, though. We can't change her, but maybe Christ will still manage it!"

"True." Taking her in his arms, he gazed into her eyes. "I married a wise woman who just keeps getting wiser as time passes."

She grinned, "Good that you know! The Lord's working on me, not to mention you're rubbing off on me, too. I'm in good company. There's just one thing I don't understand, at the moment."

"What?"

"Why aren't you kissing me, when you have me this close?"

He decided to do so, rather than puzzle over it with her.

She giggled when he took the hint.

CHAPTER 15

Whent the weekend arrived, Ted called. Erin was beside Allen when he answered, while Ruth was sitting and visiting with them. Both girls were at work. He requested prayer for Eli. Having listened to the recording of Allen's discourse on Bigfoot, the college freshman decided to research if any theories supported his. A virtual message board was utilized to post a "Bigfoot and the Bible" discussion thread.

It sounded innovative, but somehow his anonymity was pierced. The thread was spammed until he took it down. The damage was done. He had become the laughingstock of the campus. The young man was considering disenrollment.

Allen's expression disturbed Erin. She touched the side of his phone, activating the speaker, then asked for an update. Ted emphatically stated that he didn't blame Allen for the mess, but he replied he still felt responsible. They prayed together immediately.

Ruth spoke afterward, "This is the Devil at work! I've

seen it before, when he goes after our kids. It makes me so angry, I could wring his neck!"

"Is Liz aware of what happened?" Erin wanted to know.

"Not yet," Ted replied, "Eli just called me, upset. We're pretty close."

"Bring her in on it, okay?" she advised. "You *need* each other for this. Get Eli back on the phone. Both boys would be even better, then call us back. We need to take this to the Lord together!"

"Ted?"

"Yes, Allen?"

"I don't think... any good will be accomplished by Eli's continued presence at school. He's too exposed, you know? He should come home for now, I think."

"Yes!" Ruth and Erin concurred, then chuckled.

"*Thank you!* That was what I needed to hear! He'll be okay, once he's back home with us. Thank You, Jesus!"

Ted hung up to call his family. Ruth asked Allen how he was doing. He shook his head, then asked them to pray with him so God would show them what was happening and what to do. Erin held his hand as they did.

Her phone rang. It was Danielle. She had a vision of a Bible on a table, then someone reached in to place an upright miniature red flag atop it. When she prayed about it, she was impressed they needed to know. They thanked her, then his phone rang again. Ted had his family connected. Allen promised they'd clue Dani in later, before hanging up..

Liz was grateful they had Ted call her, even more so they took the matter so seriously. Conrad was, too. It was Eli who surprised them.

"I really appreciate everyone's support, but I think I overreacted, guys," he said. "A reporter from the school newsletter called a few minutes ago to set up an interview. She wants to hear my side of the story, since I was hacked.

She was sympathetic, said it shouldn't happen to anyone. If I stay here, I might get this straightened out."

There were sighs of relief.

"Ultimately, it's your decision, Eli," Allen replied. "We're all in your corner, no matter what, but can we pray first?"

He was all for it! When they finished, the telltale peace that usually followed was missing. It felt like going to bed without shutting and locking the front door, a distinct uneasiness.

"Something's wrong, bro," Conrad stated. "Has the school news written anything favorable about the Bible in the past?"

"Nothing I'm aware of, now that you mention it," Eli admitted. "It takes pride in being progressive and intellectual. The mindset here is secular and intellectual."

"This makes you, as a Bible-believing follower of Christ Jesus, an outcast and a target. You are being set up, Eli!" Allen warned him.

"You think so?" His voice was subdued, worried.

"Yes, I do. While your dad was getting you all on the line, we prayed. II Peter 3:3 came to mind, declaring how scoffers would come in the last days. They scoff at the promise of His coming, at His word in general, and at any they deem foolish enough to believe it! They are the kind of people the Lord meant when He told us not to cast our pearls before swine, lest they trample them and turn on us.

"I think this young woman wants to draw you out for the slaughter. Her sympathetic ear is meant to gain your trust, so her poison pen can assassinate your character."

Erin spoke up to describe Danielle's vision, who knew nothing of what was happening. "Does what she saw fit into all this, Sweet Talker?" she finished.

"Eli, is the message board you posted on school-sponsored?" he checked.

"Yes, it is."

"Then you weren't hacked. Any mention of the Bible was red-flagged, probably by someone on the faculty. You were anonymous to other posters, but known to those in control of the program. They have access to your registration info and exposed your identity to embarrass you. It might be tough to prove in court, but nothing is hidden from the Lord!"

"Then I'm outta here," Eli determined grimly. "*Nothing* excuses such a breach of trust!"

It was like all on the line heaved a simultaneous sigh of relief. Their collective unease was lifted with his statement. Peace was palpable.

With a deep breath, Eli chuckled, "I guess that's what the Lord wanted me to do. It's the lightest I've felt since this thing blew up!"

"Come on home, son," Liz encouraged.

Allen encouraged the young man. "There's a time and place to contend for the faith. This isn't it. This was a trap laid to destroy Christ's lambs by people who have sold themselves to do evil. It didn't work because the Good Shepherd is on the job, gathering His flock and rescuing you. He loves you, Eli, so He spared your whole family from a world of pain! That's something to think about on the way home!"

Ted was astonished. "*So much hate* on a college campus... Allen, what brings this on? They are supposed to be equipping our kids for life, not belittling or indoctrinating them. We trust them with our kids and our money, only to be spit on this way?"

"We take a chance anytime we extend our trust, Ted, especially to strangers. Christ makes all things manifest, including exposing dark motives. Whatever is in peoples' hearts, He will bring it out into the open.

"Education may put a more finished veneer on them, but it doesn't change their hearts. The same spirit who moved multitudes to demand, "*Give us Barabbas! Crucify*

Jesus!" still motivates proud intellectuals today. They believe they know what's best, even when the one they favor is the kind of person willing to stab them in the back!"

Allen turned his focus back to Ted's son. "Eli, this didn't surprise the Lord. You have time now to seek Him. Perhaps He will change your direction, not just your environment. Whatever the case, He will make you fruitful if you are mindful of Him.

"Oh, I can pretty much assure you what I shared about Bigfoot is unique."

Eli laughed.

"If you want to seek supporting theories, be careful! Don't risk your credibility discussing what won't matter until we're with the Lord. No one in this lifetime will thank you for your insights, anyway. It's for Tribulation saints, for the fiery trial *they* will face, reassuring them of God's sovereignty in the mystery of lawlessness."

"Gotcha, Allen. Sometimes I speak before I think."

There were chuckles.

"You have a bent horseshoe to show for it, too!"

Laughs could be heard.

"There's a little of Simon Peter in you, I think. Jesus had a very special relationship with him, so you're in good company. Satan wants to sift you, too, but Jesus isn't letting you go!"

"Yeah, I know. It's amazing! Thank you all! I'm gonna get packed to head home now. 'Bye!"

The family visited briefly and thanked them for their support before hanging up. They gave Danielle a call to fill her in on what happened so she would know how the Lord used her. She was bowled over, grateful to God, and appreciative for the call. She looked forward to seeing them at the upcoming wedding.

Erin received a call from Stefanie. She had been approached with an offer to buy the company! It had happened before, Erin informed Allen afterward. She and Stef passed on previous offers by bargain hunters who discounted A*C*E's fair market value.

This was different. The offer was more than double its estimated worth! It was presented by an established wrestling studio in New York. Their business was looking to expand to the West Coast. Erin's reputation appealed to them, particularly how respected she was for not faking matches. Stef was excited. In addition to buying them out, they wanted her to stay on as manager!

Erin agreed to meet with the agent during the upcoming visit. Unlike her enthused business partner, she seemed ambivalent. The company was, after all, her life's work for the better part of her adult years. Allen listened as she talked out her thoughts and feelings on the matter. He told her whatever she decided, he was fully behind her. She said that meant a lot. They began praying for the Lord's direction, asking Him to set their hearts in agreement with His.

CHAPTER 16

Being who they are, the FBI did manage to uncover records of assignments Bart Palombo carried out. Over one hundred people met their deaths prematurely at the killer's hands, according to files uncovered! The idea he had flown under the radar for so long irked Agent Cooper in a big way. A laundry list of unsolved cases was being re-examined. It would take a long time to track down the details of each one. The young redhead in Springfield had literally dodged a bullet!

Agent Gina Smythe was moved powerfully by the fact. She sought permission to go undercover and find evidence to bring charges against Heidi's mother. The young lady deserved closure, in her opinion. Her superior decided to authorize the request.

Some preparation was required to establish convincing credentials. Agent Cooper would be her contact in infiltrating the woman's business, hopefully gaining her trust. It seemed less risky than trying to pass herself off as a witch. That could be dicey.

Hilda Goins was the suspect's name. She was well known in the Los Angeles area, a famous realtor who could move property when no one else could. Her ads promised to seal the deal. Her reputation backed it up.

Agent Smythe had no problem getting work at the agency as a junior salesperson, presenting herself as licensed and having some experience in San Francisco. It turned out Hilda employed an all-female staff, except for one man, her personal secretary; *no doubt a token for the sexist company owner,* Gina reflected. His long looks her way showed an interest she thought might be worth exploiting. She passed her observation to Coop.

Everything was going smoothly, yet he was uneasy. He kept urging her to be careful until she began to tease him about it. He clammed up self-consciously, then. She showed him a ruby ring she wore on a chain under her blouse. Inside was an inscription, "From Dad, with love."

"This really is a keepsake from my father," she explained, "but it's been modified. It contains a tiny signal transmitter activated when I wear it on my finger. It will pinpoint my location for about six hours before it goes dead. If I need help, I'll put it on, okay? So stop worrying!"

Once he had its frequency, he immediately initiated the tracking program.

She chuckled, "It's too early to be concerned. I'm not doing anything risky yet."

"It makes me feel better to have it ready, okay?" he responded.

She dropped it. He was a reliable agent with good instincts and more time in the Bureau than she had. There was no one she'd rather have backing her up.

The hit man's records were circumstantial evidence against Heidi's mother. While she was incriminated, it wasn't enough for a conviction. Since he conducted his business in cash, banking records were inconclusive. They needed a record of the order being given, hopefully a text or email connecting Hilda to the assassin.

It would be easy to clone her cell phone and search the duplicate at length. Getting access to her computer would be slightly more complex. They'd have enough to make an arrest soon, she was certain. With a little luck, she anticipated notifying Heidi she was safe from her dangerously deranged parent within two weeks.

Days before the planned trip to L.A., news broke of a young Black man in St. Paul dying while being arrested by police. Unarmed and cuffed, his agitation played out as resisting arrest. The response was harsh, resulting in complications possibly contributing to the suspect's death. Multiple bystanders recorded the incident, which went viral.

A national groundswell of outrage erupted into rioting in major cities across the U.S. Though the officers involved were fired and criminally charged for their actions, the rioting escalated. The young man's name and likeness became the token for racial protests everywhere, championed largely by one particular organization with seemingly limitless resources.

The bulk of the protesters were peaceful. However, people locals did not recognize kept turning up at gatherings nationwide. They put on hoods before turning violent, smashing windows, looting businesses and starting fires. Black-owned businesses were not spared, indicating the violence might *not* be racially motivated at all!

Pallets of bricks were being left on sidewalks without explanation, inviting angry protesters to take their actions to the next level. No one knew who furnished them or any of the other weapons passed around, like guns, lasers to blind law enforcement and high-powered slingshots. Urban streets became dangerous, especially at night.

Pam and Win warned the couple, "As much as we want you here for the wedding, it would be safer to stay home."

Erin and Allen exchanged grins.

"We'll be okay," he told them. "We wouldn't miss it for the world!"

"Besides, I have business there, anyway," Erin added "The Lord will protect us."

The lovebirds were thrilled at their resolve. The rest of the brethren were, too. Fran backed them up, saying this visit was ordained for all their comfort. She confirmed God would indeed defend them on their journey!

Hilda knew something was wrong. Palombo should have sent word the job was done, yet she had no contact from him. She knew better than to call him, so she had a third party look into his whereabouts, an investigator specializing in personal information. An obituary turned up to confirm her suspicions. Bart Palombo died in a rollover in Springfield, Missouri while traveling.

Not good, she reflected angrily. Even though he was a man, he had proven useful to her more than once. Her errant offspring was an embarrassment she thought to end, but now...

She had to assume that in death, he had been discovered. An assassin crossing state lines would draw the attention of the FBI. He was cautious and thorough, the reason she employed him at times, but their resources would ferret out details that could possibly lead back to her.

Only one thing had changed from the familiar in her surroundings since the hit man died - the new agent she hired from San Francisco. Was she a mole? It didn't really matter. Better safe than sorry. She instructed her secretary to set up a meeting with the unfortunate young woman. She'd offer her a promotion and a celebratory drink, ensuring she never got to enjoy her new position.

CHAPTER 17

On approach for landing, Allen looked out the window to see a dark cloud over the Los Angeles metroplex. It wasn't the yellow-gray haze of smog always hovering over the city. This was black as night. He asked Erin if she saw it. She didn't. He described it to her and she asked him what it meant. He didn't know, but it must be some kind of spiritual oppression. They would have to pray about it.

It was Thursday afternoon when they arrived. The wedding was scheduled for 2 p.m. Saturday, but the couple intended to stay until Tuesday so visiting with everyone would not be rushed. Also, Erin and Stefanie planned a meeting to hear the purchase offer for the company on Friday. Erin wanted time to sleep on it and confer with Stef face-to-face. It was a major decision she didn't want to make hastily, then regret later.

Burned buildings were visible from the freeway, bearing witness to the unrest in the city. The couple shook their heads in amazement as they made their way to the house in their rented car. Once they exited the freeway, broken windows and spray-painted messages littered the business area they passed through. It felt anxious, with a sense of trepidation and anger radiating from people they saw.

Their welcome at the house was unusually warm, even from staff who had shown little interest in their prior visit. Juanita was there to help Stefanie with some administrative duties. She saw them first. Her face lit up as she let out a squeal! It brought others to see what was up. Laurie and Pam were thrilled to see them, but all the staff welcomed them with hugs, grins and handshakes. After the rest dispersed, Juanita, Laurie and Stef remained.

Erin asked, "Stef, how did we rate such a warm reception?"

"It's because they know you," she told them. "With the city descending into chaos at night, it's like no one knows who to trust. It's comforting to see a familiar face! Even the police don't bring much comfort. They're on edge, like they are always expecting trouble. Friendly faces have become a very welcome sight!

"I've been shutting down earlier to give the staff time to get home before they lose daylight. Even our customers appreciate it, saying they don't want us caught in a riot and getting hurt! Who would have thought? We kick their butts big-time, yet they're concerned for us!"

All four got a laugh over it.

"It's all part of the brain damage we share as guys," Allen explained. "We want to protect you ladies, even when you're tougher than we are. It's dumb, but it's how we're wired. We can't help it!"

The ladies grinned.

"You're absolutely right, dear. It *is* dumb!" Erin nodded.

"But it's also sweet," Laurie noted.

"You have a point," Stef agreed.

Erin nodded again.

Stef excused herself, saying she needed to wrap up remaining business with Pam, and Juanita entered Stef's office. Laurie stayed with them, not having anything to do at the moment. Dani was heading home from her brother's place in Oregon, updating Erin and Allen during the daily conference call fellowship meetings. She planned to be back the next day in ample time for Pam's wedding, as promised.

"So no one here has been hurt?" Erin queried Laurie. "Until we drove through town, I had no idea it was this bad."

"No, God's been watching over us. We've been praying for everyone. So far, He's kept us all from harm. Stef had a meeting when it started, warned us to avoid areas where people were massing together for no reason we could see. Apparently she's seen this kind of thing before, but you know Stef. She won't tell us when or where."

Erin acknowledged it with a short nod. Her partner had a past she wouldn't discuss with anyone, not even her best friend. She said she preferred not to dwell on it. Whatever it was, it left her with a hard edge. Allen had confided his suspicion to Erin that Stef might be capable of murder, sparked when Fran related how she was abused.

Erin confirmed his conclusion. Her friend carried a gun, a big one, and wouldn't hesitate to use it if she felt a need. Stef persuaded Erin years ago to obtain a smaller one for self-defense, then trained her how to use it. Erin became proficient, but Stef was a crack shot. Her teacher emphasized her greatest enemy was hesitation and instructed she must only draw it if she was ready to kill someone.

It sounded harsh, but it made no sense to carry a deadly weapon, otherwise. There was reassurance having it in her purse, so she kept it there and tried to forget about it. Her approach worked until Allen was attacked. She would have pulled it if she hadn't left her purse in the bedroom... and probably gotten him killed! Stef hadn't pulled her firearm for the same reason, she found out later. The realization caused her to question the wisdom of carrying a gun at all.

When he made the observation about Stef, she laid all this out to him. He didn't know she had a gun. She felt ashamed for not telling him earlier. Though surprised, it didn't upset him. She thought it might.

Allen reminded her, "Genie, your response to my plight was *perfect!* It resulted in the Lord settling the matter with no loss of life. I couldn't be more proud of you!"

Her heart soared to hear it.

"I'm comfortable trusting in Christ rather than a gun, but if you have one, maybe He has a reason for it. Unless He moves you to part with it, keep it! He directs each of us as He sees fit." Her husband reflected sheepishly, "I had no idea how I put Mom and I at risk when we first met. Unwittingly, I invited an armed stranger who was more than a match for me physically into our home. It could have gone so wrong!"

"Well, it didn't," she reminded him with a grin. "Perhaps you should have been more cautious, but no one got hurt. I'll keep the gun on one condition. You must learn to handle it safely. You don't have to practice, but for safety's sake, let me teach you how to use it properly."

He did, just to please her. It only took a few minutes. Her gratitude was expressed at greater length, making him glad he went along with her wishes!

CHAPTER 18

At the same time Erin and Allen were approaching her company headquarters, Agent Gina Smythe responded to Hilda's summons for a meeting. Her cover identity was Janet McCullough. She had been kept very busy showing houses to prospective buyers over the last ten days. It was like being caught in a whirlwind. She could gauge customer interest by their reactions, but Hilda had a hands-on approach, requiring them to call her directly to discuss terms. Her agent was to show properties and report customer interactions in annoying detail.

It was less than satisfying for a sales agent who relied on commissions for income, but Hilda had stated there would be weekly updates to let her know how she was doing.

"It's a good thing I don't count on this job," Gina told herself. *"It feels anything but secure."*

Hilda's secretary Mark greeted her cheerfully with a stare that felt like he was undressing her with his eyes. It was hard to figure him out. He seemed pleasant, a handsome well-built man with a professional bearing, yet something about him rang hollow. It was like he had no personality, no depth to him. He stepped back to Hilda's door and spoke, then turned back with a smile.

"Dame Hilda says come on in," he relayed, then returned to his desk.

"Come in, come in, Janet," Hilda bid her as she entered.

The real estate mogul was tall, like her daughter, with gray hair the color of steel. She reminded Gina of Bea Arthur. Her movements seemed almost arrogantly confident and her expressions changed too fluidly, making one wonder if any of them were sincere. Like the actress, she was a study in contradictions. Hard eyes conveyed merciless intelligence.

"You have done us proud, my dear," Hilda announced with a big smile. "How many houses have you shown in the time you've been here?"

"Twenty-three, I think," Gina smiled back. "How many sold?"

"Four!" Hilda announced triumphantly. "Four houses sold in less than two weeks' time, including that ramshackle THING on Tecumseh Drive. Did you know I've been saddled with the place for just about 75 days now?"

Gina shook her head.

"Way too long, Janet. Any residence over sixty days is way too long," Hilda explained. "You suggested remodeling the grotesque west bedroom and adjoining storage area to create a den. They loved the idea so much it became the selling point for the property! You were *born* for this business! We should celebrate. What do you drink?"

"I don't, unless I'm at home," Gina replied cautiously. "Not much then, either. Besides, I'm on a diet right now."

Hilda tsk-tsked, "Take your victories when you can, honey. I want to drink to your success. Does it have to be water, then?"

Gina grinned, "Well, at the risk of sounding picky, how about a cold can of Diet Pepsi?"

"Done! I don't drink it, but Mark does," she supplied. "Celebrating with soda. I like it!"

Hilda didn't call her secretary aloud or use an intercom, yet he appeared at the door as if summoned.

"Janet would like a cold can of Diet Pepsi," she informed him. "Just bring the can. I have glasses here." She pulled out two glasses and a bottle from a cabinet.

"Yes, Dame," he replied.

Gina rose to follow him, her training kicking in to make sure no one could drug her drink. It didn't matter. He was already back, offering her an unopened can. She took it, surprised at his uncanny speed. He withdrew without a word.

"Would you like a glass?" Hilda offered.

"No, thanks. I'm used to drinking from the can," Gina assured her.

Hilda shrugged. As she poured her drink, she chuckled. "I'm partial to Vodka, myself."

Gina surreptitiously wiped the mouth of the can with her blouse, certain her hostess didn't see how she inspected it.

As if there were eyes in the back of her head, Hilda turned to pull a tissue from a box on her desk, then offered it to Gina. "This is more sanitary, dear."

Gina blushed slightly at being caught. She took the tissue, blew her nose and discarded it. Hilda smiled, then pointedly tapped her longest finger on the desk three times as she sat. The noise was distinct.

"To my newest regular sales agent, Janet," Hilda declared, raising her glass. "No employee has ever cleared probationary status more quickly than you have. Congratulations!"

Popping open her tab, Gina drank. The room swirled

for an instant, then steadied so rapidly Gina was sure she imagined it.

Hilda rose to come around her desk and put an arm around the younger woman. "You and I are going to make lots of money together, you know?"

Gina agreed aloud as she found herself at the door under Hilda's guidance. One last smile was obscured as the door closed in her face. She made her way to her car with the thought, *"There's something really strange about that woman."*

After seeing how she spotted Gina's caution with the soda can, she realized how difficult it might be to get evidence on Hilda. She could have sworn she hid her efforts effectively, yet was caught anyway! It didn't make sense; it just didn't. As the thought echoed in her mind, which seemed a bit sluggish, she called Agent Cooper to update him.

"Must be more tired than I realized," she thought in passing.

While joining traffic on the busy six-lane highway fronting Hilda's agency, Gina called Coop.

"Hey, it's me," she announced. "I'm in! The suspect just called for a meeting to say my job is permanent now."

Agent Cooper was pleased. "Well, that went smoothly."

She chuckled, "Yeah. Apparently four of the properties I showed were sold, including one she was frustrated about. She wanted to toast our success."

Alarmed, he interrupted, "You didn't..."

"No, I didn't take any chances. I drank a can of soda that I opened myself. You know I wouldn't break protocol!" she chided him.

His sigh of relief was audible.

"I'm not green, Coop!"

"I know," he admitted. "I just worry. I won't apologize, either. I consider it healthy."

Her eyes suddenly became so heavy they closed by themselves. A tractor-trailer rig was passing on her left when it happened. When she forced them open, the rig was moving into her lane as though the driver didn't see her. She veered to her right by reflex to avoid collision -- and smashed into a pallet of bricks at nearly 50 miles per hour! Everything went black. Her phone flew out of her hand as Coop yelled, "Gina!"

CHAPTER 19

Friday's lunch meeting with the owner of the company interested in purchasing A*C*E was friendlier than Allen could have imagined. Erin wanted him with her for moral support, he supposed, and Stef welcomed his presence. He gladly supported them, but felt he had no business there otherwise. He was out of his depth as they discussed numbers and the inner workings of Erin's company.

The man introduced himself as Fred Bigelow of Bigelow Productions. He presented an offer early on far exceeding what Erin confided to Allen privately beforehand would be the minimum she would consider. The only reaction from either lady was a slight widening of Stef's eyes, indicating she was impressed. Erin kept talking terms. Allen just listened.

Mr. Bigelow wanted to include a blanket non-compete clause. Erin was willing to go along with the idea, with conditions. She would not open another wrestling-related business in California for two years after the signing of a contract, but would not be limited otherwise. After consideration, the man declared, "Fair enough."

He initially wanted exclusive rights to distribute all A*C*E videos already created in perpetuity. Erin flatly refused.

"Our videos are the result of blood, sweat and tears invested by us and people we care about. We don't begrudge including *permission* for A*C*E's new owner to profit by selling copies of our matches. However, the idea that we give up all rights to those works is never going to be acceptable! You may add your logo to the videos. No other alterations will be made, delineated as a term of the sales agreement. I have turned down offers over this issue and am prepared to do so again."

"Now hold on..." he objected.

Erin wasn't finished. "Furthermore, we're *proud* of what we created. You could potentially yank our videos off the market if you gain exclusive rights to them. I am retired, but my partner and employees have built their reputations as competitors on those works. Their future success in this field is largely dependent on people seeing what they've done so far. I will retain the right to distribute them, whether you do or not!"

Allen was impressed by her loyalty to her staff, both past and present.

It appeared Fred was, too. He laughed. "You have a point. Every video is like a part of the resume of the competitors it showcases. I make decisions concerning what to promote based on sales and what profits the company, but the ladies' careers are directly affected by what the niche market we serve sees. Okay. If you want to go on selling, I'm not thrilled, but as long as you don't undercut our prices, perhaps we can reach an agreement."

Frankly, Allen was shocked! The man seemed determined to make a deal.

Erin smiled sweetly. "Mr. Bigelow, I don't want to

compete with you if you buy us out. All I want is to retain enough rights to protect my ladies without going to court, should the worst happen. I've learned to be very careful how I conduct my business, that's all. Once one gives up his or her rights, there's no going back, as you well know."

The meeting continued until the man excused himself, saying he had to consult his partners, but didn't foresee any difficulties in what was discussed.

Erin rose to shake his hand. "I don't really have much motivation to sell, Mr. Bigelow. We're quite happy with things as they are. We'd be fools not to consider every opportunity as a matter of course, however, and nothing you said was a deal breaker, all things considered."

His eyebrows arched in surprise. "I *will* be in touch," he promised and left.

She sat down, appraising her partner and her husband. "So what do you two think?"

Stef was aghast, "Are you kidding? Erin, he's offering double what the company is worth! Why are you hesitant?"

"Well, I guess that tells me where you stand," Erin chuckled.

Stef grinned and nodded. Both ladies looked at him.

"You really want my opinion?" Allen asked. When they nodded, he gave it to them. "The company belongs to you two. You built it and invested your lives in it for years. I honestly don't feel I have any right to weigh in on your decision. If I share my thoughts, it's only because you asked, okay?"

Both smiled. Erin gripped his hand in encouragement.

He shrugged, "Okay. I don't know what his angle is, but Bigelow seems determined to make a deal. Genie, I fully expected him to get up and walk out on us while ago."

Erin nodded.

"I can't explain why he didn't. You may not be motivated to sell, but his motivation to buy A*C*E more than makes up for your reticence. I think if you ask for half again what he offered, he'll meet your demand."

Stef's eyes went wide as saucers.

Erin nodded slowly. "I had the same impression."

"You can't be serious!" Stef practically exploded. "This is a great opportunity, sister. If you up the ante and he withdraws, you're going to kick yourself! We'll both miss out!"

"Possibly," Erin admitted, "but if he is willing to go along with it, you'll pocket nearly one point five million more. Maybe that's worth the risk."

Stef was speechless at the thought.

"Let's sleep on it," Erin proposed. "If the three of us don't agree on this matter by Sunday, we won't ask for more. Time out until then?"

Stef grinned, "I can't refuse your offer, even though it won't change my mind. I have to admit it's fun to think about! You want to make a gambler of me, eh?"

Erin shook her head. "For some reason, I don't think it's a gamble, Stef. We can only sell the company once. If God is giving us favor with the buyer, we might as well seek a windfall! If it doesn't happen, we won't lose anything we didn't have yesterday, right? As I recall, we were satisfied then."

Stef rose with a chuckle. "True enough. I need to get back. If I sit here longer, you might just talk me into this!"

CHAPTER 20

U sing GPS to find his partner's phone, Agent Cooper
arrived on the scene before rescue personnel
finished extricating her from the car. He was
informed she was alive, though bricks coming through the
windshield left her battered and unconscious. When she
arrived at the hospital, it was determined she had sustained
multiple concussions, facial lacerations and a broken ankle.
The attending physician said swelling of the brain was his
foremost concern. He wasn't certain she would survive.

"She'll be in intensive care for at least 48 hours," he
told Coop. "You can sit with her and talk to her. It might
help. She's not conscious, but her babbling is surprisingly
coherent. It's just babbling; she doesn't know what she's
saying. Don't expect a response until the swelling starts to
subside. We're monitoring for seizures or vomiting that
could lead to asphyxiation. Are you expecting any other
visitors?"

"No," the Agent replied.

"Just as well," the doctor said. "You're allowed one

more to stay and two for five minutes or so, but you'll have to step out whenever staff needs room to work."

"Understood," Coop acknowledged.

Bandages covered much of her face, but he could see it was swollen. Multiple monitors were hooked up, along with an IV and oxygen. He shook his head, wondering how all this happened.

She appeared to be asleep, but a word slipped out, "Coop?"

"I'm here," he assured her and took her hand. There was no response. He remembered the doctor said it was unconscious babbling. He settled in a chair beside the bed. Their investigation was done. A new effort might be launched, but Gina was key to this one, and she was out of commission. He hoped it wasn't permanent!

"Coop?" she asked again. Her eyes didn't open. There was no sign she was awake.

The reply came out naturally, "I'm right here, Gina." Again there was no response. *'Hoo boy, this is gonna be a long night,'* he thought.

"Call Heidi," she instructed.

'Where did that come from?' he wondered. "If you can hear me, Gina, I can't. It's not protocol." Still no response, no indication she could hear him. He settled back, getting comfortable.

About ten minutes later, she spoke clearly, "No accident, Coop. She wants me dead!"

The words chilled him. He was sure the "she" Gina spoke of was Hilda, but how? Did she somehow follow his partner and run her off the road? Only Gina could testify if it were so. One thing he was suddenly certain of -- she wasn't rambling. Perhaps she couldn't hear him, but the words she uttered were like messages in a bottle, one after another.

As he put it together, she spoke again. "We need help. Call Heidi."

This time he didn't answer. He waited for more in vain. She didn't talk at all afterwards, though he stayed close all night. When they took her a little after 10 a.m. for an MRI, he left to eat and freshen up. He returned as they brought her back, still unconscious. The doctor came in to examine her, then turned to Coop.

"It's not looking good," he announced. "She should be regaining consciousness for a few minutes here and there, by now. We haven't seen any hemorrhaging, which is good, but there's nothing more we can do until she wakes up. You might want to notify next of kin, just in case." He left the room.

Coop reeled at the news!

Just then, Gina spoke matter-of-factly, "Heidi can help. I will die if you don't call her, Coop!"

It was the last straw. Tired and rattled by the doctor's words, he pulled out his cell phone, checked the file and called the young redhead.

"Hello?" Heidi answered hesitantly.

"Sorry to bother you," he started. "This is Agent Cooper of the FBI. Do you remember me?"

"Oh! Sure, I remember. I'm surprised to hear from you. What's up?" she asked.

"Well, my partner Agent Smythe has been in an auto accident. She's in intensive care. The doctor isn't sure she'll survive. She's been unconscious since the collision yesterday."

He could hear the young lady's intake of breath.

"The doctor says her words are simply unconscious rambling, but she keeps telling me to call you. She just told me her life depends on it. I don't know what she expects you to do, but I can't ignore her and live with it if she passes away, you know?"

"She's talking without knowing what she's saying, you say?" Heidi pinpointed.

"Exactly. She hasn't regained consciousness, doesn't

respond to me at all."

"You went after my mother, didn't you?" the young lady intuited.

"I'm not allowed to discuss an ongoing investigation... Oh, hell! The investigation can't continue now," he declared in frustration. "Yes. Gina - Agent Smythe - was undercover and making progress, until THIS happened!"

"Then it wasn't an accident," Heidi asserted. "Strange as it sounds, she's been cursed! I wish you had listened to me. Mother is dangerous in ways you never dreamed a person could be. You're in Los Angeles, then?"

"Yes," he replied defensively. *'Cursed?! What kind of a nut is this girl?"* he thought. Then he remembered her mother claimed to be a witch. She probably raised her daughter to be one, too. "You're not going to tell me witchcraft will help my partner, are you?"

"No way! Witchcraft put her in the hospital, Agent Cooper. The power of God that rescued me is her only hope now. I'm going to get people praying for her. Do you remember the older couple I live with, Allen and Erin Edwards?"

"Yes, I do," he answered.

"I trust them with my life, literally," she declared. "They are in L.A. for a wedding right now. If I give them your number, they'll call and most likely come visit. My dad - I think of them as the parents I should have had, growing up - knows how to come against evil in the name of Jesus Christ."

"I don't believe in such things," he interrupted.

"I understand," she acknowledged, "but what alternatives do you have? Sounds like there's nothing else you can do. Isn't it worth a try?"

He deflated, no argument left. "Have them call me. Heidi? Thank you."

"No problem. I'm already praying."

CHAPTER 21

Erin received Heidi's call right after lunch on Friday. On speakerphone, their girl explained what Agent Cooper told her.

"Agent Smythe is in trouble," she finished. "It's mother's *modus operandi*. She either knows or suspects what Smythe was doing. A suspicion is enough to motivate her! The curse she levied against the agent will keep attacking her until she's dead, unless the Lord intervenes. I don't know how Smythe put together calling me would help."

"I don't think she did," Allen observed. "If the doctor is convinced it's just rambling, I think the Lord made use of her voice as a witness to her partner. Ultimately, it's God's decision whether the lady lives or dies. Everyone's time is in His hands. Apparently, He has decided this isn't hers. He wants to save both of them, instead!"

"Praise the Lord! I told Cooper I'd give you his number, so he's expecting your call. Are you gonna go see them?" she inquired.

"Yes, we will," Erin supplied, looking at Allen.

He smiled and nodded.

"Will you bring everyone in our fellowship up to speed so they will be praying with us?"

Heidi indicated she would.

"We'll let you know how it goes, sweetie."

"Thanks," came the reply. "I'll text you his number. Love you guys! 'Bye."

They called Agent Cooper to find out where to meet him, then headed out from the house where Erin's company was headquartered. On the way, Erin questioned Allen.

"I understand witchcraft is real from our experience with Heidi, and demons are definitely real, but *curses*? I thought that was superstitious baloney, Sweet Talker. Do they really have any power?"

He answered, completely serious, "Yes, as much as the Devil can empower them. He can only do what God allows him to do, though. Sometimes curses are overruled, rendering them void outright. Whoever receives Christ is covered by His blood. Under the authority of His name, we can break them, but they harass us until we do.

"If we don't recognize them for what they are, we can be troubled for years before we specifically take authority over them, one by one. A blanket declaration of freedom isn't specific enough to break an individual curse. We need the Lord to reveal what we face.

"For the unsaved, curses can be deadly. They are defenseless against them. The reason I think Agent Smythe was mindlessly urging Cooper to call Heidi is due to God's compassion. Seeing they were defenseless, He put words in her mouth to call our girl, knowing what it would initiate. Smythe wouldn't understand how calling Heidi would help, and therefore wouldn't knowingly urge her partner to call. Only God knew, so He intervened on their behalf.

"He could have done so as a sovereign act directly, but they wouldn't know what happened. He wants to highlight

Christ so they can be saved, so He brought us into the matter to bear witness of Jesus! That being the case, it's clear the Lord won't allow this curse to gain victory in the end."

Erin grinned, "So she won't die, but get saved instead? Wow!"

Allen smiled back, "I think He's planning along those lines. The choice to receive salvation is still theirs to make. When Arum used Heidi to attack me, you didn't know if I'd survive, but you told God you trusted Him to resurrect me if necessary. The same possibility exists for Smythe now, along with the same choice Heidi had to make afterward."

"That's powerful," Erin replied, amazed.

"Yes, it is. Remember the outcome, though? Not only was Heidi saved, but Laurie was, too. A steady stream of salvations has been taking place ever since. The origins of the family gathered in faith around us hearkens back to God's display of power on my behalf. Now, He has orchestrated similar circumstances around these two FBI agents! Only He knows what the ripple effect will be, but WE know from scripture *"His word does not return to Him void."*

She turned into the hospital parking lot, praising the Lord for His grace. Agent Cooper waited at the entrance, more disheveled than when they first met him. He shook their hands.

"Thanks for coming," he said earnestly. "I can't say I have confidence in prayer, but it's nice to have supportive people with us, under the circumstances."

"It's our pleasure, Agent Cooper. Even if you don't believe in prayer or God, what we do isn't going to hurt anything," Allen pointed out.

He smiled, "True. Call me Coop; all my friends do. Gina's this way."

He led them to her in the ICU, explaining hospital policy would not allow two visitors to remain beyond a few minutes. The couple agreed to make their prayer brief. They did so, laying hands on the injured agent, going into tongues for a bit after specifically declaring the works of the Devil against her null and void, in Jesus' name. Not a word came out of the patient's mouth while they were there, nor did she stir. Coop decided to have a cup of coffee with them before they left.

Agent Smythe was lost in darkness for what seemed like forever. She couldn't move, wouldn't have known which way to go if she could. There was a weight on her she couldn't identify until light began to filter in around her. Her eyes felt like they opened by themselves. She was in a bed with equipment around it, perhaps a hospital bed. Her attention was focused on the weight pinning her. It was horrifying.

A rat the size of a German Shepherd slavered atop her body. It peered down with greedy human eyes, malicious and intelligent. She wanted to scream! Her mouth opened, but no sound came out. The rat raised its head, then deliberately spit into her open mouth! She started to gag.

Two figures glowing with white light appeared at her bedside. The rat leapt off her, running from the bright human-shaped figures in a panic. One of the figures pursued. First the rat, then the pursuer went through the closed window like it didn't exist. Her attention was drawn back to the remaining figure.

Holding her forehead gently but firmly, his fingers went into her mouth. She couldn't feel it, already gagging from the rat's phlegm. With a scooping motion, the glowing man extracted a wad of brown goo the size of her own fist. She gasped for air, able to breathe again! Disgusted, the man flung the goo into a trash can before looking back at her, his hand lightly resting on her forehead once more.

He began to speak. "Prayers were made on your behalf, prayers heard by God Most High. He dispatched us so you would not die at this time. He decreed you shall live! We'll stand guard to enforce His decree while you recover, Gina. Rest and listen closely to the gospel of Jesus you'll soon hear. It holds the key to your salvation. We wish to see you obtain it!" A smile as big as Texas covered his face as he faded from view. Her eyes closed on their own.

Minutes later, a nursing assistant entered to take vital signs. A putrid smell derailed her intent, causing her to utter "Eeww!" She found the source in a trash can beside the bed, apparently vomit. She checked the patient's lips for traces, concerned she might aspirate, but found nothing. Remembering this patient had not woken once since being brought in, she summoned the nurse.

While they conferred, Gina woke. They were startled when she spoke. "Where am I?"

The assistant left to get the doctor. The nurse answered her question and asked how she was feeling.

"Okay, I guess, just sore," she replied.

The doctor came in and a quick examination followed. He appeared simultaneously pleased and perplexed. The nurse showed him the vomit.

He turned back to Gina. "Did you raise up and vomit into this can?"

"I don't think so. I don't remember," she replied.

When the nurse tilted it so she could see, the memory of the rat and the glowing men came back in a rush. She turned white as a sheet!

Wrongly interpreting her reaction as nausea, the nurse apologized and instantly turned away, discarding the trash bag and replacing it with a clean one. It didn't matter. Having seen its contents, she knew her dream must have been real!

The doctor explained about the auto accident leading to her hospitalization and revealed the extent of her injuries. Coop came in while the doctor was talking.

"You had multiple concussions at the time of your arrival, Ms. Smythe. Lacerations and a broken ankle were also sustained, but only the concussions were life-threatening. Every hour you were unconscious increased the likelihood you would not recover.

"Now, I'm not seeing evidence of a concussion at all! I want to run another MRI to be sure, but if the results confirm it, you'll leave me with a mystery. And I do mean leave! There will be no reason for you to take up space in the ICU anymore. You might even be discharged tomorrow! A broken ankle is scarcely a reason to keep you."

He left her with Coop. He had such a grin on his face, it infected her.

"What are you so happy about, Agent Cooper? Were you that worried?" she asked.

"Gina, the doctor told me to contact your next of kin. *HE* was that worried about you."

She looked surprised.

"If you hadn't demanded I call Heidi, I think we'd have lost you. Allen and Erin..."

"I did what?" she interrupted, confused.

"You don't remember?"

She shook her head slowly. "Remember what?"

Coop settled into the chair, taking a deep breath. "I guess you really were out of it. The doctor called your words meaningless rambling. You urged me over and over to call Heidi, saying she could help. Today you told me you would die if I didn't. Then the doctor came in, checked on you and tried to prepare me for that outcome.

"It was too much! Agency protocols be hanged! I couldn't live with myself if I let you die without doing what you asked of me."

"I don't recall asking, Coop. I'm sorry I put you in that position," she acknowledged.

He chuckled, "I'm not. I'm convinced it saved your

life! Heidi concluded her mother cursed you."

Gina's eyes went wide.

"She promised to get people praying. The older couple she lives with - remember Erin and Allen?"

Gina did.

"They're here in L.A. for a wedding. Heidi called them, then they called me. They were HERE a little more than half an hour ago, Gina, to pray for you."

Her jaw dropped, remembering the glowing man who saved her from choking stated he and his companion were sent because of prayers on her behalf! Tears began to flow as staff rolled in to transport her for the MRI. They asked him to step out, but she stopped them a moment before he did.

"I have something to tell you too, Coop. Will you wait for me?"

He replied with a nod, "I'll be here."

CHAPTER 22

Back at her house, Erin and Allen were relaxing together, having just returned from the hospital. Allen's phone rang almost as soon as they arrived. It was Coop, cluing them in that Gina was awake and apparently out of danger! An MRI was underway to provide confirmation, but the doctor said he no longer saw signs of concussion. Coop wanted to visit with them tomorrow, but it might have to be somewhere else. It looked as if Gina might be discharged!

Allen congratulated him on the good news and welcomed a new meeting. When they hung up, he told Erin what happened. Both thanked God for answering prayer as Erin sent out a mass text with the news and thanked everyone for their prayers. Allen called Heidi personally to update her, as promised. The young lady was thrilled the Lord used her in this matter, along with how He answered their prayers.

Her excitement had Allen chuckling. "Just when you thought you were sidelined, the Lord put you back into play, didn't He?"

Hearing it, Erin nudged him and put her hand to her ear. He activated the speaker phone.

"Mom's on now, too," he announced.

They exchanged greetings before Heidi responded, "I can't believe it! I've been feeling like I was useless for anything important, you know? Helping Miss Ruth is important, too, but not really exciting. I guess I was resigned to expecting mundane things, a mundane life, then the Lord brought me into this! I feel so... honored!"

"Oh, Heidi, He's not gonna forget you," Allen reassured her softly. "We may not be sure of our own worth sometimes, but Jesus' scars are proof how much He values each of us, including you."

"We're proud of you, sweetheart," Erin added. "You did good."

A sniffle could be heard.

Allen reminded her, "God trusts you, daughter. You never forget who you trust. It's even true of God himself! He's coping with an angelic rebellion, remember? Satan's revolt highlights the value of servants the Lord notes are trustworthy. You know all too well how precious trustworthy companionship is, having been betrayed by your mother and Arum!"

Another sniffle was heard before the emphatic response, "Do I ever! I don't think I would have survived it without you two and this new family God made of us. I see your point, Dad. I'm not perfect, but if Jesus is counting on me, I'll do my best not to let Him down!"

"There you go!" Allen encouraged. "Don't forget, He treasures your service, even when it seems more mundane than exciting. It will all be rewarded when we see Him!"

The couple was reminded of Stef's policy change when freshly-showered staff started passing through the living room on the way home about 4:20 p.m. Several mentioned they'd see them at the wedding tomorrow, while some just said goodbye. Laurie and Dani, back from her trip, settled with them, asking what their plans were for the evening. Pam joined them as they thought it over.

"Actually, Win and I were hoping you would join us for dinner," she declared. "You came all this way for our wedding. We'd like to spend some time with you, and we'll be occupied tomorrow. Stef, you'll be our guest too, won't you?"

"Delighted," Stef responded with a smile.

Laurie looked uncertain until Pam turned to her and Dani. "I realize I'm not Emily, but you're short a musketeer. We can't have that! How about you join us, and I'll sub in her absence?"

The gymnast lit up, nodding emphatically.

Dani replied, "I think you just made her night! Thank you."

"What do you have in mind?" Erin inquired. "Is this limited to invitations only? We'd hate to exclude any who'd want to join us, you know." She looked at Allen, who vigorously nodded agreement. "We're happy to offset costs, by the way."

"I get it," Pam chuckled. "This isn't exclusive. We reserved a room at a buffet in the mall near Win's office, big enough to accommodate our whole near family in Christ! We never intended to monopolize your time, just surprise you. It only seems spontaneous. The truth is, we've already invited the rest of our fellowship."

Allen's and Erin's eyes widened.

"Win and I liked the idea of spending our last night as singles together with all of you, rather than wasting it with bachelor/bachelorette parties away from each other. Why commemorate loneliness when we can celebrate with friends we love?" she finished.

Laurie applauded in delight.

Dani shook her head in amazement. "That makes so much sense! Pam, you want Allen and Erin to write instructions about relationships, but I think we're already gaining insights from you and Win, too!"

Pam smiled and shrugged.

Laurie exclaimed, "Yes! Full speed ahead. No looking back, when you know what you want!"

Allen stood, then stepped behind the excited young lady and placed his hands on her shoulders. She looked back at him curiously as he addressed Pam, "If you wonder where your cheering section is situated tomorrow, just look for Laurie. We'll be gathered around her!"

Laurie giggled as Pam responded, "No doubt!"

Win arrived just before 5:00 p.m. and led the group to the buffet where they held reservations. A sizable side room was set aside to host their gathering, which was fortunate, because everyone but Andrew showed up by six! He texted Win he was working late, but hoped to arrive soon. Tom and Carol were the last in the line, citing that they had to bar the windows and doors of their cake shop. God had spared the area around the business so far, but they were taking precautions, just in case.

Erin and Allen were welcomed with delight. There was enthusiasm as they all came together. Several expressed it felt like a family reunion. The couple concurred, bombarded by hugs as they were. After the group was settled, trays loaded with everyone's selections set before them, the doors to their reserved dining area were closed to give them privacy. Thanks was given for the food, then Win rose to address the guests.

He began, "Pam and I thank you all for coming, from the bottom of our hearts. Neither of us has ever felt such a bond of love as we do with you. It's amazing, considering the short period of time we've known many of you! On the eve before our wedding, we are glad to celebrate with our household in Christ. We don't regret our lives as singles, but they have brought us to this juncture, which we eagerly embrace. Why waste time bidding farewell to a lonely life when we so anticipate what's ahead?"

Enthusiastic applause answered him.

He continued, "For those of you who wonder if you'll ever find that special someone to share your life with, please remember you're not on a solo mission. It isn't chance or happenstance guiding your lives; it is the Lord Jesus Himself! It took nearly forty years to arrive at this point in my life. Looking back, I see now how He was bringing me to this moment all along."

He offered his hand to Pam. She took it with a smile and rose to stand beside him, her eyes never leaving his face.

"I didn't know Him to trust Him until recently, but His timing was perfect. Had Pam and I met earlier in life, my immaturity would have scuttled any relationship the two of us might've had. I've come a long way! My mouth still gets me in trouble sometimes, but not like it used to. I had no filter and much more ego than appropriate!"

His statement was greeted with laughter.

A wry smile tugged at the corners of his mouth. "It's ironic that the woman who holds my heart specializes in breaking the will of prideful men! Let's just say it reinforces my determination not to return to my old ways!"

Pam smiled as the room chuckled.

"Anyway, if God's timing was so perfect in bringing us together when much of our lives went by without knowing Him, I guarantee His timing is working on behalf of you who trust Him now. He knows how you desire love and companionship. It matters to Him, and He'll bring it about in due time with a partner you can trust. If He did it for me, He'll do it for you, too!"

Applause filled the room. Allen and Erin stood clapping, followed closely by the singles, then all the rest joined them. When it died down, the focus was on the food, though a hum of conversations accompanied the feast. Andrew had slipped in quietly halfway through Win's speech. Settling next to Fran, they exchanged a smile, then the big man gave the dentist a huge thumbs-up following the applause.

Stef ribbed Allen, "Looks like there might be another speechmaker around here to steal your thunder! Are you okay with that?" A little smirk and the twinkle in her eye accentuated her teasing.

Erin wore a sly smile when she looked at her mate to see his reaction.

"I don't mind a bit, Stef," he came back. "Kind of feels like I've been given the night off! I love seeing everyone encouraged. As far as I'm concerned, all of you are my family. It fills me with satisfaction when any of you are blessed!" He raised his voice a bit to address their host, "You did good, Win!"

Erin clamped a hand above his knee with a slight smile and a shake of her head.

Pam beamed at her man.

With a shrug, Win replied, "I just spoke from my heart, Allen."

The older man confirmed, "That's how it's done!"

Nothing weighty was discussed. It was just friends enjoying each other's company, laughing, joking and having a good time as they celebrated the upcoming nuptials. The answer to prayer for Agent Smythe earlier also had the group in high spirits.

When God answers prayer, it's a joyful reminder that our wishes *matter* to Him, that *we* matter to Him. The cross of Christ made the point once and for all, yet being insecure and forgetful, we need constant reminders. He knows and supplies what we need, spoon-fed morsels of grace, tokens of His affection to get us through life. There are some needs we never outgrow.

Laurie finished her plate quickly, then urged Dani into a spontaneous gathering with Pam. After a short, low-tone discussion that had Win chuckling and Pam shaking her head with a smile, Pam rose to address the room.

"Win and I didn't have plans beyond dinner with all of you; just getting together was our main focus. As you all know from our shared testimonies, each of us benefits as members of this family in Christ.

"For some, though, who suffered the loss of a familial connection in the course of life, this new connection has a deeply personal value. It provides a kind of support they were denied in their formative years. Erin and Allen have given of themselves so freely that some, like Laurie, have adopted them as immediate family.

"It's a good thing, too. Aging retirees are likely to need some younger people to take care of them as they become feeble, you know!"

Shocked laughter erupted as Erin's and Allen's jaws dropped.

Laughing at her own words, Pam added, "I'm living dangerously now!"

"Yes, you are," Erin warned.

Laurie was laughing, blushing and backing away from Pam. "I didn't put her up to that, Mom, I promise!"

"Maybe not, but you're still laughing," Erin pointed out with a hint of a smile.

"I can't help it!" Laurie protested. "It was funny!"

Dani didn't say a word, just laughed with everyone else.

Recovering her composure, Pam declared, "In the absence of Heidi and Emily, I offered to fill in as one of the three musketeers, as they call themselves. Laurie and Dani may not welcome me the next time if they see I bring trouble down on us! Anyway, Laurie wants to play mini golf, says it has become a family tradition. Win and I are up for it. What do y'all think?"

Most nodded in approval.

Allen spoke up, "Win, your tendency to put your foot in your mouth is rubbing off on Pam! Are you gonna be a bad influence on her?"

The dentist laughed, shrugging.

Allen turned to Erin and asked, "Why isn't anyone worried about offending ME?"

She grinned, "Because we all know what a sweetie you are, love. Bluffing doesn't work if you haven't intimidated or kicked someone's butt. Besides, one heartfelt hug is all it takes to undo any playful offense heaped on you. We all have your number!"

He nodded ruefully, "I'm too transparent, I guess."

"Maybe," she replied, "but we relax with you because of it. We trust you enough to be ourselves. Not many people make us so comfortable in their presence."

Nods all around indicated silent agreement.

"Mini golf, then," he pivoted.

Laurie exhaled, "Yes!" which brought more laughter.

"There's enough of us to make four groups, looks like. The course will think they're hosting a small busload.."

CHAPTER 23

They didn't have to go far. The mall they were in had mini golf outside, as it turned out. There was a heavy security presence that watched gatherings closely for signs of trouble, determined to keep mallgoers safe and comfortable. The result was a thriving business for shops and businesses on the property, including the course. It was busy, but the group was able to play.

Scorecards were designed for up to six people per group, so they divided into four groups. Those were impeded by smaller groups wanting to play through, which made for slow going. It was tedious.

Halfway through, an employee approached Win in the first group with an offer. The facility had three courses. If the entire party was willing to break off their game and wait a few minutes, one course would be designated just for them, and they could start over. He gladly accepted the offer.

The party was sidelined less than five minutes before starting anew. Without being rushed, they were able to watch each other play. The fun factor skyrocketed as they rooted each other on, cracking up laughing when strokes went awry! Half a dozen would play the hole, then watch the efforts of the next batch until all had finished and were ready to move on. Watching the others was half the fun!

Andrew was uncanny. He said he never played before, but he walked each hole to get the layout, then just seemed to know how to beat it. His claim was hard to believe, though he insisted it was true. Allen joked it was the altitude. Andrew had a birds-eye view. Combined with a steady hand, he racked up a score a pro would be proud of; no one else even came close.

Reina had a blast! She told Carlos she wanted to be included whenever possible in future games. She would make time to play! Juanita and Laurie assured her they would get her out with them. Carlos and Dani agreed, laughing and shaking their heads.

Guillermo's attention was on Denise. She was trying to give him pointers, but giggles kept breaking her concentration. He wasn't helping her get it together, either! Clowning around and making silly faces, he enjoyed entertaining her.

Fran cast several amused looks their way. She, Teresa and Stef buddied up, with the unlikely addition of teen Alissa. Allen was surprised, thinking she would prefer to stay close to her parents, but something about the middle-aged women drew her.

He pointed out his observation to Erin. She smiled, whispering in his ear she'd explain later. Eli and Conrad were accompanied by Erik, generously including him in their talk and play.

The nucleus of the group consisted of four couples: Allen and Erin, Hans and Alma, Ted and Liz, and Tom and Carol. Win and Pam was with them, paying close attention to their interactions, relaxed and staying close. Those four couples encouraged and joked with each player as their turns came up; it was plain to see how they fed on the attention. Their stability, anchored in the marital bonds they shared, drew the rest back to them again and again in delight, building an atmosphere of joy.

As they finished up the first game, Allen inquired loudly, "Are we doing this again?"

The resounding "Yes!" of many voices nearly blew him off his feet. He stumbled backward as Erin caught his arm.

He grinned at her sheepishly, "I guess I asked a silly question."

There was a wave of laughter as they set up to go again.

Stefanie moved in close, having heard him. "Yeah, you did, but don't feel bad, 'cause I've got one, too! This is about as pointless a game as anything I've ever seen, guys. So WHY am I having so much fun?"

It evoked more laughter.

Allen had no answer, but Andrew did. "I don't think it's the game we're enjoying as much as the company around us, Stef," he rumbled.

"You've got that right," Reina chimed in, "although I happen to like the game, too."

They played two more rounds before going their separate ways. Liz, Alma, Carol and Conrad all thanked Laurie for suggesting the activity before they left, which brought a bright smile to her face. All reassured Win and Pam they planned to attend the wedding the next day.

Erin detoured for ice cream before taking Allen back to the house. She gave her take on why Alissa was drawn to her partner and the others. "Teens establish their identity by choosing role models, Sweet Talker," she told him. "Alissa is at the age when kids begin to break free of their parents and start setting goals for themselves. Teresa has helped her get out and explore what choices are available to her.

"She could do a lot worse than looking to my business

partner for inspiration! Stef isn't just physically impressive, she's a successful career woman who carries herself with confidence. She's articulate and independent, qualities a young person desires to cultivate in his or her self.

"Fran thinks she's weak, having come to the end of herself, but she has turned out to be resilient in ways I think she has overlooked. She struggled to fight for herself because she didn't know how and wasn't sure she was worth fighting for! However, under the right circumstances, I think there's a mama bear inside her who would fight tooth and nail for the people she cares about. As the Lord uses her to minister to others, her determination and resourcefulness in Christ will surprise her more than it does anyone around her, in my opinion. Alissa may sense that inner strength."

Allen shook his head, looking at her in wonder, "Wow! Thank you for explaining this to me. I agree one hundred percent with everything you just said, but I doubt I would have put it together on my own. You're absolutely right! There's a lot for Alissa to admire in both of those ladies. I believe your assessment of Fran is right on! I wonder if Alissa admires *you*? I think she could learn a lot from you. I know I do."

She gave him a crooked grin, "I appreciate that, Sweet Talker. I learn a lot from you, too. It thrills me to face life beside you! She has her ears open, taking in everything around her, me included, but I have you. She is single, so strong *single* women probably seem more relevant to her right now."

"That makes sense," he replied.

"It's not just a thing with young people, either," she pointed out. "No matter how old we are, we're always looking for people to admire and emulate. It's part of trying to better ourselves. Caught up in the process, we may miss how others are looking at *us*, like how Pam watched us tonight, or how most all those guys watch you!"

"Okay, let's not go there, please. I'm self-conscious enough already!"

Erin giggled mischievously, "Yeah, I know the thought makes you uncomfortable, but it's true. You're worth emulating! Don't worry about it, just be yourself. No effort is needed on your part. It's Jesus in you they admire and love. He won't fail them." She patted his knee and he heaved a sigh of relief, covering her hand with his.

When they reached the house, Stef was waiting for them in the living room. "What took you so long?" she asked curiously.

"We stopped for ice cream," Erin responded briefly as she and Allen settled on the couch.

Stef smiled, shaking her head, "I should have known. Not a bad idea, actually." There was a hesitation. "I wasn't kidding," she added. "I *really* had fun. I waited here for you because... I wasn't ready to be alone, if that makes sense."

"Well, that's good, since we noisy houseguests are back to shatter your peace and quiet all over again," Allen observed with a grin.

Both ladies burst out laughing.

"You just can't seem to get rid of us. Every time we go home, it doesn't last. We keep coming back!"

Erin picked up where he stopped. "Yeah, it's like I just pretended to leave. Instead, I keep returning to displace you from your bedroom, dragging Allen along with me so you'll have to throw both of us out, not just me!"

Stef was laughing hard, tears running down her cheeks.

"Bet you never guessed this house was coming to you fully furnished, complete with chronic invasive squatters!"

"STOP!" Stef begged, so cracked up she labored to catch her breath.

The couple complied, grinning and chuckling.

Trying to get it together, she gasped, "You... That's not right!" Drying her eyes and blowing her nose, she shook her head. "How can I feel sorry for myself when you do that?"

Allen touched Erin, getting her attention. "Is that her plan? I never agreed to cooperate with it. Did you?"

"Huh-uh, no way," she deadpanned. Turning to look at Stef, she declared, "We don't like your plan. You should probably make a new one so we can get on board."

Stef snorted, "Just like that, huh?"

The couple nodded.

Erin asked seriously, "Stef, you don't talk about your feelings much. Does loneliness bug you more than you let on?"

"Not usually, but occasionally it gets to me," she replied. "Win's speech kind of hit home. His reassurance probably meant something to the other singles, but I don't share your faith, so God is no comfort to me. With my history, which I'm not willing to go into now, the idea of a soul mate I can share life with doesn't seem possible. I am alone. It's overwhelming at times." She winked at Allen. "Like you said, you guys are "somebody" for me when those times come."

Erin stood and went to her with a full embrace, which was returned with interest.

Allen commented, "What did I tell you, Genie? She is just so *needy*!"

Stef shook with laughter as they separated.

Erin turned to rejoin him, a small smile on her face as she admonished him, "Behave, orneriness."

He grinned as she held his hand affectionately. "Maybe I better quit pushing my luck, at that. She's liable to be counting down the days until I'm out of her hair."

Stef shook her head emphatically, "Nope! You challenge me in a way you'll never regret, Allen. I'm too serious sometimes. You're good for me. You two are like a medicine for my dark moods. The day is coming when I'll share where they originate. In the meantime, just know you both mean the world to me, okay?"

She stood. With a nod their way and a simple "Good night," which they returned, she headed for the bunk room and shut the door.

CHAPTER 24

Something between a mist and a drizzle was coming down the next morning when they got up around 8:30 a.m. Laurie and Dani arrived with breakfast burritos slightly before 9:00, wanting to be present for the 10 a.m. phone fellowship and just hang out. Stef joined them for breakfast, then headed for the weight room. They held a Bible study and prayer meeting, asking in particular for a blessing on the nuptials ahead. They also thanked God again for His answer to their prayers on behalf of Agent Smythe, as well as keeping everyone safe last night while they were out.

According to the news, there was a group of three to four hundred people who marched for several blocks near city hall the night before. They were dressed in black, wore hoods, and chanted, "Death to America!" It didn't even fit with the supposed cause of the riots. making it plain other forces were at work beyond racial tensions.

Allen remembered the dark cloud he saw over the city when they arrived. He told those on the phone about it when the news became a topic, then explained it indicated a spiritual onslaught against their nation. They came against it in prayer, together.

With things to do, Win and Pam had to go, but others wanted to discuss matters further. Ted led off, "Allen, is all this a smokescreen to attempt to overthrow our government? I just thought it was a renewal of racial tensions, like the protests that marked the 1950s and 1960s. That's before my time, but it seemed like growing pains as the nation tried to root out bigotry."

Allen replied, "Ted, you're not wrong about that time, but there's always been more to it. Racial discrimination had to be addressed. Much was eventually made right, but ethnic differences are intrinsic to America. This nation's strength has been in reverent recognition of the grace God showed us, even before we became a nation. Jesus is our strength, who has broken down the walls dividing us to make us equal before Him and equally dependent on Him.

"America is the melting pot of many races, when it functions properly. Each race has its strengths and weaknesses, but like an alloy, we strengthen each other when we come together as one. We don't lose our identity by coming together, we gain another facet in embracing our place as Americans, not in pride, but humbly before Christ Jesus, our Redeemer. We do it to please our Savior, but we benefit from this unique identity.

"Therefore, Satan's strategy is to attack the bond holding the nation's alloy together. He emphasizes the differences between us, attempting to paint some as victims. then uses whatever he can to offend and turn us against each other. Enemy nations deliberately fan those flames into hatred and unreasoning anger, too. America has the capacity to be the backbone of what is good in this world, as it was through two world wars when the populace reverenced God and scripture.

"Many have turned away from Christ since then. That

has left the nation wide open to every temptation and Satan is exploiting all of them, ruthlessly. America needs to turn back to God if it is to continue walking in freedom, or it will fall.

"The rise of the Antichrist is at hand. He *needs* this nation's resources to form a revived Roman Empire. No other nation has so many bases and outposts on foreign soil. Scripture indicates no nation on Earth has the strength to withstand him, so America's fall is a sure thing, eventually."

"You're not making me feel better, Allen," Andrew protested. Several voices muttered uncomfortable agreement.

"Don't you think we're smart enough to see through the Devil's ploy?" Eli contended.

Allen sighed, "It's never been about how smart we are. Sometimes, the smartest people do the dumbest things! It's about IDENTITY. Knowing Christ causes us to learn who we are in Him, and we act accordingly. Think back on your walk with Him. How many times would you have done things differently if pleasing Him didn't matter to you? His desires have replaced your own as your motives in life, haven't they?"

There was acknowledgement expressed for the point.

Allen continued, "It is much easier to deceive people who aren't certain who they are. Identity is established through the father in a household, just like our Father in Heaven established our identity in Christ Jesus! That's why every member of the family bears His name. It gives us belonging. It's also why Satan has belittled fathers and worked so hard to split up families. It leaves the kids floundering, trying to discover who they are and sometimes even *what* they are, the reason gender confusion has become such a big deal!"

"Whoa, I never thought of that!" Fran breathed in surprise.

"Me neither, but it makes sense," Reina declared. "Laurie, I think I understand why you call Allen your dad now."

"He accepts me. He loves me and he's proud of me," she replied. "I never had that, growing up. I don't know if there's anyone out there like him, but if there is, I'm going to marry him!"

There were chuckles, but Laurie was absolutely serious and didn't laugh.

Allen reassured her, "Well, I'll never stop loving you, sweetie, even when you do!"

She giggled, "I know, Dad. I love you, too."

He addressed Eli, "Have you ever noticed how protests tend to generate on college campuses? Knowledge is exalted there, while young folks are trying to figure out who they are and who they want to be, their identity. It's easy to guide opinions if certain knowledge is spotlighted while other information is suppressed; colleges and news media do it all the time. Mark my words, all this unrest will be acted out at the universities, sooner or later. That might even be why the Lord led you out of the one you were enrolled in, to protect you."

"Thank You, Jesus!" Liz blurted out.

"Yes, Lord," Ted added.

"I'm sorry if what I said made you uneasy, Andrew," Allen told him. "If it helps, I don't think the globalist power grab will be permitted to succeed before Jesus raptures us out. He declared the gates of hell will not prevail against His Church. As long as we're still here, I believe that protection extends over the only nation in history founded on His grace! Once we're extracted, though, the world will quickly absorb what remains of it."

"Thanks, Allen. That does make me feel better," he admitted.

There were sighs of relief on the line. Hearing it, Allen led them in a prayer for peace before the call ended.

Dani and Laurie enjoyed having Erin and Allen all to themselves afterward. They were dressed for the wedding and planned to ride with the couple, so they wouldn't have to rush around as the time approached. Erin made sandwiches for lunch there at the house, keeping things simple. The risk of messing up dresses was minimized, in doing so. She and Allen changed after eating, then the group left for the ceremony.

On the way, Allen got a call. Agent Cooper said the doctor reported the MRI showed no signs of concussion. He couldn't explain it, but the results were undeniable, so Agent Smythe would be released in the late afternoon. They planned to fly back east on Monday, but his partner wanted to talk with them before leaving. Could they meet with them tomorrow?

Allen told them no problem, but they would likely not be alone, as their time in the area was limited. Was that okay?

Coop chuckled, "Well, we won't be discussing state secrets, I guess."

Allen laughed.

"Gina saw something she wants to discuss with you. She told me and I'm curious, too. With her leg in a cast, it's not like we can go play tennis, so meeting with you will probably be the highlight of our day."

Allen clued Erin in and she suggested meeting over lunch. A restaurant was chosen and a time set. As he hung up, he noticed a strange expression on Dani's face.

"Is something wrong, sis?" he inquired.

She shook her head, looking a bit bewildered. "I think I saw this coming, Allen. If it happens like I think it will, we'll end up back at the house with them. I'll have something to do and something to say to total strangers that's outside my comfort zone. If it happens, will you all stay close and make sure I don't mess up?"

Laurie took her hand and smiled encouragement,

nodding.

"Of course we will!" Allen assured her.

"We've got your back," Erin promised.

CHAPTER 25

T he wedding was comfortable, unusually so. Win and Pam were all in on the commitment to share their lives together; there were no wedding jitters anyone could see. The minister was a military vet who ran a mission for the homeless downtown. Well-known and respected throughout the city, he was one of Win's first patients. Thrilled to hear his dentist had committed to Christ, he jumped at the opportunity to conduct his wedding. He prevailed on a pastor acquaintance to borrow his church for the ceremony, a moderate-sized facility capable of seating nearly four hundred people.

Good thing, too! Close to three hundred attended; both bride and groom had extensive families and many friends. Allen, Erin, Dani and Laurie arrived early, so they observed how the sanctuary filled up. Allen shook his head.

Erin noticed. With a grin, she inquired, "Aren't you glad they didn't ask you to marry them, too?"

Wide-eyed, he replied, "Very! This would be overwhelming!"

The younger ladies smiled.

Erin held his hand and joked, "Can't have that! Overwhelming you is my job!"

Laurie cracked up laughing, while Dani grinned knowingly.

Allen blushed.

"Just enjoy being a spectator this time, love," she finished.

Heaving a sigh, he nodded.

Their friends from the night before settled around them as the crowd grew, and the ceremony went off without a hitch. There was no mistaking the joy on the newlyweds' faces!

When their little fellowship reached the front to congratulate them, Win introduced them to Brother Nowicki, the presiding minister. Tall and imposing, he had long hair tied back in a ponytail and wore a brown suit with a bolo tie. He appeared to be in his mid-forties.

He greeted them enthusiastically and shook Allen's hand. "So you're the man who led the Doc to Christ? Then I'm a big fan of yours, Mr. Edwards! I've been witnessing to him for years without success. He listened politely, but nothing I said persuaded him. What's your secret?"

Allen replied with a chuckle, "Please, call me Allen. I don't have one, Brother. I just answered their questions the best I could and recommended they investigate Christ's claims together. Getting together seemed to appeal to them; that's how they ended up here today!"

There was laughter from those standing by, particularly the happy couple.

"You planted the seed of God's word and I watered it, but Christ gave the increase. Let Him have the glory. He deserves it!"

Several "Amens!" were uttered in response.

The man looked surprised. "You're not trained as a minister," he stated.

Allen shrugged, saying nothing.

He nodded slowly, "Yet you're anointed, no question. There's more to you than you're admitting, Allen. Would you object to me sitting in on some of your conference call meetings?"

"As long as you're respectful and not disruptive, I'm good with it. There will probably be doctrinal differences arising between us in time. We can discuss those outside the meetings. Not to be catty, I'm just extremely protective of these folks. They have bared their hearts to each other. Letting their trust become a liability is utterly unacceptable to me."

The finality of Allen's tone raised several eyebrows among those with them.

Brother Nowicki smiled. "Spoken with the heart of a shepherd! I can't help but respect you for it. Good enough. My name is Glen, by the way. See you at the reception!"

He turned as others sought his attention.

They worked their way out to the parking lot, where Carlos stopped. "Mr. Allen, I never heard you get so firm before. Do you think he's a threat to us?"

"If I did, Carlos, I wouldn't welcome him, not even to sit in quietly," Allen assured him. "I don't know him, though, so it's best if expectations are clear."

Laurie observed, "We guard Dad, but Dad guards us, too. It all works out!"

Smiles were all around them as they parted to go to the reception. Dani was still curious, though. Once the four of them were rolling, she inquired, "Will Glen be allowed to speak when he's on the line with us?"

Allen was in the front passenger seat; Erin was driving, but looked at him for his response.

"Of course he will," Allen smiled. "Have I ever shushed anyone in our fellowship meetings?"

Three heads shook emphatically.

"Everyone deserves respect, to be heard. How else

would we get to know him? But that must take place before he gives any instruction. Being a minister, it may take conscious restraint to keep from falling into the habit. He may have something useful to add to us, but we must know and trust him first. The Lord will bear witness of everyone who belongs to Him.

"It works the other way, too. As he gets to know us, the Holy Spirit will reassure him Whose we are, as well. His response will indicate the effect it has on him: either he'll love joining us or decide we're not his kind of people. He seems curious about me right now, since I'm not traditionally trained in ministry, so he'll evaluate what I teach and probably test me with some questions. There's nothing wrong with that," he added.

"Not to put you on the spot, Sweet Talker, but have you received any training in ministry?" Erin reminded him, "You told me you were called and it was hard to define, because it didn't fit any traditional sense. You don't seem to have the polish in your manner other preachers display, yet your - he called it "anointing" - is plainly genuine. God is with you. It only takes minutes from meeting you to recognize it!"

Laurie and Dani were on the edge of their seats, following Erin's train of thought closely.

She wrapped it up, "All of us came to Christ after you came into our lives. That didn't just *happen*. You must have had some preparation before getting to this point in your life."

He thought over how to explain it.

She apparently thought he was reticent, so she motivated him with a sly look. "Am I going to have to interrogate you to get my answers?"

The ladies in the back seat were plainly confused, but Allen jumped, looking at his mate warily. "N-no," he replied hastily, then explained, "No, I was just thinking how to respond, that's all. It's a fair question. If anybody is going to put me on the spot, Genie, I prefer it to be you, because you care about me."

She lit up with a bright smile.

"This ride isn't long enough to give you more than a basic answer, though, so here goes. Many years ago, long before we met, the Lord told me He would train me Himself. His exact words were *I don't want you confused by the knowledge and lack of knowledge men have.* That's why I never attended a bible college or seminary. He led me into scripture, opening my understanding and giving me a personal revelation of the gospel. For three and a half years, nearly every spare moment and all my lunch hours at work were spent immersed in the Bible and time with Him.

"The result was that my knowledge of Him and His word increased dramatically, but so did my dependence on Him for direction and comprehension of scripture. He became my Source and my most intimate Friend. For me, ministry is just sharing with others what I have with Him! I don't know how to be a professional minister, which is what I would have learned from men. Jesus wanted me to depend on His Spirit, instead.

"It is the way of the world that professionals achieve success. God never saw it that way. In Revelation chapter three, He assessed the church at Laodicea as lukewarm, unacceptable, and on the verge of being rejected if they didn't return to Him. I asked what makes a church lukewarm. This was what He said, *The slide of churches into mediocrity began when ministry became a profession, rather than a stewardship.*

"A profession is how one obtains livelihood, but stewardship demands accountability. He has *servants.* He doesn't hire professionals to run His Church, He appoints servants.

"The world demands church leaders be educated according to standards it sets. If church leaders don't measure up to their standards, society withholds recognition of their legitimacy REGARDLESS of how effectively the Lord works in their midst. His validation should always be the final confirmation of whether a movement is His. Glen is open-minded enough to see for himself whether Christ is working in me. The vast majority would decide against me, simply because I'm not one of them."

"That's not right!" Laurie declared indignantly. "I got saved 'cause of you. We all did!"

"Jesus knows," Erin reassured her, "and that outweighs whatever others think they know. He's the Gatekeeper to heaven, remember? He'll let us in."

"Exactly!" Allen concurred. "He knows us. Whoever is turned away will be told, *I never knew you. Depart from me, you workers of iniquity!* Higher education neither qualifies nor disqualifies from ministry, ladies. It is the call and anointing of God that's pivotal.

"Every church reflects the authenticity of its ministers. Their training is empowering in some ways, but there's a temptation to lean on it and neglect prayer. Scripture warns us to trust in the Lord and lean not to our own understanding, lest we stray. The more one understands, the bigger the temptation to take the Lord for granted.

"Is this making sense? It would be considered hogwash in secular churches, and outright rebellion by the majority of established ministry. They have man's approval, but many will be shocked when they stand before Christ. That's why I'm constantly looking for His approval. I prefer to seek chastening, rather than find out later I ran in vain. I don't think I could stand to hear Him say that!"

Dani gripped his shoulder reassuringly; Laurie followed suit a moment later.

"We're only part of the proof you're on the right track, Allen. You were obedient and you love us like He does. How could He not be pleased with you?" Dani asked.

"I think I get it, Sweet Talker. Those taught to present

the kingdom of God like silver-tongued salesmen may well overlook their own need to enter it. Is that about right?" Erin checked.

He nodded and smiled as she patted his knee, turning them into the parking lot. They had arrived.

An event facility at a hotel was the site chosen for the reception. Their own fellowship gathered loosely around Erin and Allen, visiting with each other. The newlyweds arrived twenty minutes later. Punch was served and guests were seated at long tables set in rows in a huge room.

Toasts were made and the cake was served while Win's best man, his older brother, entertained the crowd with stories of how they grew up. His take on their misadventures had the crowd in stitches, especially Pam. When she looked at him in disbelief, he just shrugged, a cheesy grin on his face. It seemed the tales were true!

It was 5:30 p.m. by the time the newlyweds departed and the festivities ended. Stef also left with a short farewell to Erin. Nothing had been planned to follow the reception, but everyone was hungry, so Erin invited their friends to join them at the food court of the mall they visited the night before.

She admitted a sub shop there appealed to her, but they could pick whatever sounded good to them. Quick and informal made a nice counterpoint to the afternoon, so the invitation was well-received. Way more seating than they needed made it easy to accommodate their number.

Over dinner, Allen told everyone of the call received from Agent Cooper and the subsequent plans to meet over lunch the next day. When he looked at Erin, she nodded with a smile and he invited the whole group to join them. Having invested time in prayer for Agent Smythe, they were excited to meet them and see what God had done for her!

Carol had a concern. "Won't it be kind of off-putting if we all show up for this, Allen? Our numbers could put them on the defensive, don't you think?"

Several faces reflected concern at the idea, turning to hear the response.

"Good question!" he praised her. "In some cases, that might worry me, too, but I told him we'd likely have loved ones around us we don't often get to see, since our time here is limited. They've been through the wringer, sister. It might be encouraging to see how many have been praying for them and meet y'all personally, you know?"

"That's true," Denise put in. "Even if they're unsaved, surely it can't hurt to meet strangers and discover they're rooting for you. God did something good for them when they were in big trouble! It will encourage us to hear it and them to know we're on their side, too!"

"Couldn't have said it better myself!" Allen told her, getting a big smile in return.

When dinner was finished, the group parted, eager to change out of dress clothes. Erin let it be known she'd be enjoying a swim in her pool after the food had settled and invited any who wanted to join her and Allen.

Allen was surprised. "When did I say I'd be going swimming tonight?" he asked.

"YOU didn't; I did," she informed him smugly. "If I'm getting in the pool, I'm taking you with me, and that's all there is to it!"

Shocked grins and some giggles resulted from those around them.

"You likened me to a shark, remember? Well, I plan to play with my tuna, Sweet Talker, so you best plan to get wet!" Seeing him blush, she took his hand with a mischievous smirk. "Besides, you can't refuse me. I'm irresistible to you, remember?"

"Yeah, that's true," he admitted.

"Pool party!" Laurie announced loudly with a huge grin.

CHAPTER 26

Not everyone attended the fun, but most of the younger folks participated. Hans and Alma brought their kids, who had a blast! Andrew escorted Fran; Guillermo and Denise met them there. Of course, Laurie and Dani were there, too. Carlos waded at the shallow end with Juanita, who wanted time in the water, but was cautious, taking no risks with her pregnancy.

The rest played hard and wore themselves out. By 9:45 p.m., everyone had left. Allen and Erin found themselves alone. According to a text Erin received, Stef was gone for the night. Allen wondered aloud what she did during her unexplained overnight absences, but Erin had no clue. The two of them talked and cuddled in bed until falling asleep.

He woke the next morning to a text message from Laurie at 8:20 a.m. It read, "Breakfast??"

He laughed, explaining to Erin when she asked about it. She shook her head and smiled as he called his 'adopted' daughter back on speakerphone.

"I got your message. Are you offering to cook?" he

inquired.

Erin chuckled.

"Huh? Oh, no! I was hoping you might," she answered quickly. "I'll pick something up if you don't feel like it, though."

"It's a kind offer, but we'll figure something out," he reassured her. "Does anything sound good to both of you?"

He looked at his partner.

Erin replied, "I'm easy, but I wonder if Laurie has something specific in mind?"

"Well, how about Southwest Scramble? Is that okay?"

Erin laughed, "I knew it!"

Allen smiled at her and she gave his hand a squeeze.

Laurie dissembled, "Truthfully, I'd be satisfied with oatmeal, as long as I'm with you guys. The food isn't really that important."

"Then come on over," Allen encouraged her. "We'll share hugs and food."

Erin nodded.

"Remembering last time, I think I better ask; are you bringing anyone with you?"

There was a mischievous giggle. "Actually, I intended to invite Dani, Juanita and Carlos to meet me there. Is that okay?"

He looked at Erin, "Why does she want to ambush me?"

Another giggle was heard.

"Because she knows you're a good sport, Sweet Talker."

She addressed Laurie, "You'll need to bring two cans of Rotel and a dozen eggs, Sweetie. I think we have the rest of the ingredients here. Can you make it by nine? Lunch isn't that far off, you know."

"On my way, Mom. Thanks!" She hung up.

"I guess I'm making Southwest Scramble," he commented wryly.

He was sitting in bed, having risen up while on the phone. Erin thrust him down and pinned him with a grin.

"Oh, come on, now," she challenged him. "Were you really gonna refuse her?"

He gave her a small smile that let the truth be known.

"Yeah, I know you. There was no chance of that happening. Our youngest has you wrapped around her little finger! You might as well admit it."

He looked up at her and shook his head. "I hadn't thought about it in those terms, but I guess you're right. I blame you! You saw what was happening and did nothing to stop it!"

She snorted, "As if I could! You're such an emotional basket case, you can't help giving all your love away! I'd have to lock you up to stop it, you big softie!"

He chuckled.

"I'm not willing to do that, so I stand beside you, learning to live with the fallout." She leaned down, her face inches from his, and her tone softened. "You know what else? I'm so proud of you I could burst! Words will never express how much I love you, my Sweet Talker. Let's go get ready."

She got up off of him, then helped him up with a smirk.

"Besides, we need to brush our teeth so I can kiss you. That's the price you pay for being mine!"

Once the objective was reached, he set the record straight. Shaking his head, his eyes fixed on hers as they held each other close, he disagreed.

"Nuh-uh, I'm not forfeiting anything by being yours, Genie. I am so *privileged* you're willing to have me. Your affection isn't a price I pay, it's a perk I enjoy. I can't get enough of it!"

The response was a long deep kiss that ended abruptly when she shuddered and stepped back.

"We're getting ready for something, all right, but not

company!" she observed. "We need to focus and come back to this later. Agreed?"

He did. Good thing, too; Carlos, Juanita and Laurie arrived all at once barely fifteen minutes later. Dani took another ten. They ate leisurely before initiating their conference call fellowship. Time flew by until they had to hang up to make their lunch appointment with the FBI. All four visitors rode with them to the restaurant.

Erin reserved a room for their party when it became apparent how many planned to attend. Pam and Win were absent, on their honeymoon, and Heidi and Emily obviously couldn't make it. Ruth heard what had happened, though, and requested via Heidi to be kept up to speed in the matter. She was very curious to hear how God answered their prayers for the agents. Erin promised to pass along whatever they heard.

When the six of them arrived about fifteen minutes early, they were ushered into a room with seating for thirty. Over half the seats were already occupied! Unmistakable enthusiasm radiated from their friends, eager to hear what God had done in response to their prayers As the rest of their party arrived, so did Agents Cooper and Smythe.

Even though they had previously met only Allen and Erin, Agent Smythe's crutches were a dead giveaway as to their identity. Spontaneous applause became a standing ovation. Allen waved them over to settle beside him at the head of the group. The agents' faces expressed wonder at the greeting they received. Agent Cooper's voice was drowned out by the noise, but the word "Why?" was plainly formed on his lips while his partner settled gratefully.

Allen stood. Reaching for Erin's hand, she took his and stood beside him with a smile. He motioned for silence before speaking.

"Agent Cooper, everyone, and Agent Smythe," indicating each with a gesture.

He nodded acknowledgement and she waved briefly.

"We haven't mistaken you for rock stars, just so you know."

That brought laughter from the crowd. Agent Cooper settled beside his partner, still listening closely.

"When you called Heidi on Friday, she told you she would get people praying for God to intervene on your behalf. Even if you didn't believe in Him then, those who responded do. This is the majority, though not all, of those who petitioned God for you in Jesus' name. Our hearts go into our prayers. We invested ourselves in seeking your well-being, if that makes sense, even if most of us didn't know you.

"Seeing Agent Smythe safe and out of danger thrills us! Our God provided what we requested. We're filled with joy to see you're okay with our own eyes, which is why you received such a welcome."

Heads nodded everywhere in agreement.

The agents noticed. Their eyes widened as they realized the whole room fully supported them.

"Our investment on your behalf has bonded us to you," Allen summarized. "No one in this world wishes you well more than we do. Am I right?" he asked the crowd.

Enthusiastic applause indicated he was.

The Feds were speechless, looking at each other. His head shook slightly. A single tear ran down her cheek.

When the applause died down, Agent Cooper gathered himself and spoke loud enough for the room to hear, "Th- thank you, all of you. We're not used to receiving popular support, and yours couldn't have come at a better time. Prayer doesn't make sense to me, but yours accomplished something we desperately needed. For that, we can't thank you enough."

He looked at his partner questioningly. She still looked disorganized.

Erin broke in, "We'll get back to this, but in the

meantime, staff is waiting to take our orders. Let's not keep them waiting!"

A group of wait staff by the entryway began to circulate amongst the guests. Restaurant service took center stage for a while. Drinks arrived, then appetizers, and finally plates. Agent Smythe was quiet, but attentive to conversations around her - and to her food.

A smile appeared when Allen commented how she must have suffered with the hospital food, to be enjoying the current fare so much.

Agent Cooper outed her, "No, Gina isn't shy. She has lots to say, so she's getting lunch finished before she dives into it, that's all. She wanted this meeting, remember?"

Agent Smythe gave a big nod. Looking at Allen and Erin, she said between bites, "Yep. Coop knows me too well. This is definitely better than hospital food, though!"

She finished while many were still working on theirs. Nursing a glass of iced tea, she asked Allen and Erin if it was okay to begin.

With nods from many, they bid her to go ahead.

"You people caught us by surprise," she began, her voice raised to reach all corners of the room. "We never expected such a warm welcome from strangers. It capped off the weirdest weekend we've ever experienced! What a pleasant turn of events! Since we are among friends, please call me Gina."

She glanced at her partner, who nodded, then added, "You can call him Coop; all his friends do.

"His experience and mine over the last three days have been very different. We've had time to compare notes. It has raised questions we can't answer. Maybe you can," she looked at Allen.

"These things are beyond the agency's scope, so only the facts will be reported. You will not be mentioned, as we can't satisfactorily explain your involvement! Witchcraft and prayer would not be taken seriously by our superiors, so we'll leave all that out."

There were nods of understanding among her listeners.

"However, I'm convinced my survival is due to the intervention of a higher power. His servants told me so to my face! They said prayers were offered on my behalf, YOUR prayers - and they were granted. I can't set that aside. Thank you all, from the bottom of my heart."

She paused. Fresh applause broke out.

She laughed when Guillermo shouted loudly, "You rock, Gina!"

A wave of laughter broke out, and even Coop grinned.

"I don't know about that," she replied, "but thank you. I will relate what I experienced, but Coop will have to fill in the blanks. I'm told I was comatose, so there are a lot of those. After a meeting Thursday under my cover identity, I was driving back to base when sleep suddenly overwhelmed me. It defies explanation. I was driving, then - nothing. I felt an impact like I slammed into a brick wall, then nothing at all." She looked over at Coop.

With a wry smile, he stated, "Close. It was a pallet of bricks that had no reason to be there. Gina was on the phone updating me when it happened. I knew something was wrong when her voice was fading. There was a loud bang and the connection was lost. I used GPS to find a rescue crew extracting her from the wreckage and followed the ambulance to the hospital."

A clink of dishes being removed by wait staff seemed loud against the silence. Even though twenty-five were present, not counting restaurant staff, they were already immersed in the tale. The staff looked apologetic when she drew attention, but smiled in relief when Allen gave her a thumbs-up. Several others followed his lead.

"It was there I received stark news. Loose bricks coming through the windshield had caused multiple concussions. Swelling of the brain posed a real threat to her life. Facial contusions and a broken ankle would heal in time, IF she survived.

"Her doctor said it all hinged on her waking up. He was worried when it didn't happen. By Friday about noon, he advised me to contact next of kin, because it looked like she would not survive."

CHAPTER 27

A sharp hiss of intaken breath came from his audience over the doctor's words.

Coop continued, "I left something out. He advised me early on if Gina spoke while unconscious, it would only be mindless incoherent rambling. When she did, it *wasn't*. She urged me to call Heidi, whom we had met in the course of an investigation. That's not protocol. I tried to explain why I couldn't, but I couldn't reach her to reason with her."

Gina inserted, "I have no memory of it. I believe you, I just don't remember."

"I understand, but it was pesky enough to fit your personality," he chuckled.

She laughed.

"You worked on me all night, pushing me to call Heidi. I was worn out by the next morning, when the doctor advised me to contact your next of kin. Then you pressed the idea again and told me you would die if I didn't!

"It was too much. I couldn't live with refusing you, should that happen. Protocol be hanged! I have to live with my conscience, so I called."

"I assume you folks know Heidi better than I do, since she's one of you, so what she said might not seem as outlandish to you as it did to me."

Smiles of understanding lit his audience's faces. Allen, Erin, Laurie and Dani wore proud grins.

"She said Gina had been cursed, an act of witchcraft. She promised to get people - you people, I guess - praying for her and put me in touch with these two," indicating Allen and Erin with a thumb. "They came to pray for her in Intensive Care and comforted me. I had no clue how badly I needed it."

"When I returned, Gina was awake! The doctor was at a loss, saying he could find no evidence of concussions diagnosed beforehand. He ordered another MRI. When it came back clean, he kicked her out of the ICU and ordered twenty-four hours of observation before releasing her.

"There's more, but it's her story to tell. I filled in the blanks, partner," he turned to Gina. "Back to you."

"Thanks," she replied. "At some point, I became aware of being surrounded by darkness. It was the first sensation I felt since falling asleep at the wheel. The second was a weight pressing down on me, making it hard to breathe. My eyes didn't open easily, but when they did, it looked like I was in a hospital bed. It was confusing because I didn't know how I got there, but that was the least of my concerns when I saw what was on top of me!

"A *rat* the size of a large dog was crouched on me, slavering in my face and crushing the wind out of my lungs! It had intelligent human eyes staring into mine. It *knew* what it was doing. I opened my mouth to scream, but I couldn't draw enough air to make a sound. It deliberately spat a wad of something nasty into my mouth the size of my fist. I gagged and choked, realizing I was dying. The thing on me actually smiled as it watched!

"Then two glowing men in white appeared beside the

bed. The rat fled in terror as one of the men pursued, both going through the window like it wasn't there. The bigger man stayed. Holding my head still with one hand, he reached into my mouth and pulled a wad of foul goo out of my throat. I could breathe again! With a look of disgust, he flung it into a trash can and released me.

"Too exhausted to do more, I listened as he smiled and spoke comforting words. He said prayers had gone up to God Most High on my behalf. In response, He decreed I should live and not die, dispatching him and his companion to see to it. He said I was safe now and they would remain with me to make sure of it. He told me to rest, saying I would soon hear the gospel of Jesus that offers salvation. He declared he and his companion were eager to see me obtain it!

"I fell asleep then, waking when I heard someone enter the room. Staff was checking on me, I guess. The woman got excited when I spoke to her and went to get a nurse, who must have called the doctor. They asked if I vomited. I didn't know what they were talking about until one of them held up the trash can with the stinky goo in it. That's when I realized it wasn't just a dream. It all really happened!"

The room stirred as praise was offered to the Lord and some applause broke out.

Gina continued, "I wish I had the presence of mind to have them save the goo so it could be analyzed."

"It wouldn't have mattered, Gina," Allen replied. "I doubt anything definitive would have come of it, anyway. A wad of mucus would have been sufficient to kill you in your weakened state, which was the purpose of the curse. It's broken now; that's the important thing. The threat is past."

"So, is that what a demon looks like? If I hadn't seen it myself, I never would have believed such a thing was real."

Finding Allen was willing to try to provide answers, she was focused on him. The rest of the room was, too.

"Not really, no," was his short answer. "Scripture speaks of heaven, hell, angels and demons to people who accept the reality of God and the truth of His word. For others who aren't prepared to take the Bible to heart yet, I'll attempt to lay out the truth in more scientific terms. Please remember I'm not a scientist, so my translation may leave something to be desired, okay?"

The audience peered at him curiously, uncertain what to expect. Gina nodded.

Coop smiled and replied, "Okay. I'm not sure if it will work, but we appreciate the attempt."

"Fair enough. We live in a three-dimensional universe where things have height, width and depth, right? That's the material reality. Our senses note these dimensions, but we instinctively know there must be more.

"Energy comes and goes, unaccounted for. Effects like wind seem to have no source. There is a balance to everything, far too carefully established to be random. It predates the rise of mankind and continues outside of our control, yet we couldn't live without it.

"One big example is our atmosphere. Primarily nitrogen, there's enough oxygen to sustain life in a fine balance. A few percentage points less would suffocate all flesh and blood creatures, while a few points more would ignite the planet, turning it into a cinder. Do you follow me so far?"

Nods and affirmative verbalizations indicated he hadn't lost them.

"Popular theory is that life on earth was seeded by extra-terrestrials long ago. It doesn't explain how all these vital balances are maintained, though. They are looking in the wrong direction. The beings still working amongst us are extra-dimensional, not from outer space. The spiritual realms of the Bible are where those beings live.

"It's been postulated there are actually twelve dimensions. Only God fills all twelve simultaneously.

Humanity lives in three, so we're pretty limited. Those who occupy more than we do function outside our perceptions. When we do detect them, our brains are overloaded, so they project images of themselves we can accept, or maybe our brains simplify what we perceive so we can handle the input. I'm not sure which it is. It could be a little of both.

"Truthfully, I don't think you saw a demon, but I'm certain those glowing men were angels. They bore witness to God, their Master, as proper servants would, so they are His holy angels, not numbered among their fallen rebellious kin. Remember how Heidi said you were cursed? I think what you saw atop you was a form of the curse, itself."

The audience, their own fellowship, sat back in amazement. Gina nodded slowly, thinking. Coop's expression was inscrutable.

Tom spoke up, "Allen, I've never heard of such an idea. Where do you get all this?"

A rueful half-smile on his face, Allen shrugged, "From the Lord, I hope. I could be wrong. You all know me; I'm only human, but I give you the best I have. So far, the Lord has kept me from serious error, as far as I know. There is a passage where He promises His own *no weapon formed against us will prosper.*"

He turned back to Gina, "That curse was a weapon formed against *you* by the Devil's forces. It was given a form of temporary semi-life to complete its mission, to kill you. The closest thing I can liken it to is a programmed robot assassin, only having an occult nature, rather than electronic. The angel you watched pursue it would not have stopped until he overtook and destroyed it."

Coop spoke up, "If I were to accept all this - a big 'if' - that would mean there exists an extra-dimensional technology far beyond our own. Can you quantify that?"

"Not definitively, no, but signs are everywhere. UFO sightings don't make sense, otherwise. Those objects perform maneuvers that ignore natural laws. Being who you are, you probably know more about such things than I do!

"Can we create a celestial orbit around Earth that doesn't degrade for thousands of years without needing corrections? Yet the moon does just that! Why doesn't the sun burn up or blow up without regulation of its activities? If it were fully stable, would there be occasional flares? Yet it continues as we need it to, and has as far back as memory goes!

"I realize it stretches the imagination, but the word of God itself is technology the world cannot fathom. It's not surprising, then, if some of His creations who have watched Him work have learned some impressive tricks of their own. If they have more dimensions to work in than we do, their feats would seem godlike to us, don't you think?"

Gina nodded slowly, "Coop is playing 'Devil's advocate', Allen, but you're right. We know more than he's letting on about some of these things."

Coop scolded her, "Gina!"

"Hey, you told on me a while ago, remember?" she tossed back over her shoulder, then looked back at Allen. "We can't talk about state secrets. I wish we could."

She cocked her head curiously, "Do you think those two angels I saw are still with me?"

A huge grin lit his face, "Yes, absolutely."

She looked puzzled, "How can you be so sure?"

Laurie and some of the younger folks perked up, looking around like they hoped to see them.

"Because they told you so, Gina, and God's holy messengers would never lie, because God hates lies. They said they'd stay with you. You will hear the gospel of Jesus Christ, the very hope of salvation, and they want to see you obtain it, remember?"

Fran called out with a grin, "The Bible says the angels of heaven rejoice when one sinner gets saved. You two can make their day!"

Gina shook her head and smiled, "Well, after they saved my life, the least I can do is listen. Is there somewhere we can go where I can get more comfortable? This chair is getting hard to take."

CHAPTER 28

L ock, stock, and barrel, the entire group adjourned to the company house. The reception area held everyone in reasonable comfort, as Erin's folding chairs were padded and more inviting than most. Gina was situated on the lone couch with her injured leg elevated. Andrew was provided a dining room chair to support his weight once again. Coop placed his folding chair beside Gina and the couch, in case she needed anything.

Once everyone was situated, Gina noted the unusual nature of the house.

Erin explained, "This isn't used just as living quarters. It's a business, primarily, converted into studios for recording wrestling matches. My partner and I hire young ladies, training them to grapple with men willing to pay for the opportunity to take them on. As we practice constantly, we're accustomed to winning, forcing our hapless customers to submit to our expertise over and over. Knockouts are also an option, along with occasional pins."

"Really?" Coop questioned, not looking convinced.

"You get enough business to pay the bills, doing this?"

"There's more," she explained. "We record the matches and sell them as downloads on the internet. That's our chief source of income, truthfully. Of course, our longevity has accumulated a loyal clientele over the years, and I've worked hard to build a reputation for fair play and not cheating my customers. The result is we stay busy."

"Well, I can see how your premise would draw men," Gina observed. "This background is the last thing I expected to hear from people who prayed for me. I guess I thought you might be a church or something."

"We're something," Allen interjected. "We're a movement of the God who saved your life. He saved ours, too, bringing us together to worship and witness of Him, while supporting one another. All of us have suffered wounds in the course of life that still challenge us, but these friends help us to keep going. Their care comes without criticism. I can't tell you how much it means in a world that loves to point out our shortcomings."

Both their guests nodded in understanding.

Erin picked it up again, "The movement started with me. God showed Allen to me in dreams before we ever met. Nightly dreams for three years acquainted me with a tender-hearted man I could easily break, but found I didn't want to. He respected, loved and honored me in ways I never experienced in real life. Imagine my surprise when I met Allen for real on a cross-country trip!

"Visiting with him for less than two hours caused me to realize two things. First, he didn't just resemble the man in my dreams; he WAS that man, mannerisms, heart and all! Second, somewhere in all those dreams, my imagination was captured. I was already so in love I couldn't stand myself! He didn't know it, but there was *no way* I would let him get away from me," she pointed out with a look his way.

He chuckled and smiled.

"He didn't, either," she smirked in satisfaction. "I had to slow my roll quite a bit so he could keep up with me, but he was worth it! As we became acquainted, his belief in God and the Bible challenged me. I looked into it while the miles separated us. If it had been anyone but *him* motivating me, I wouldn't have changed, but I was determined to have him in my life. Realizing he mattered so much to me, I committed my heart to the Lord to be with Allen.

"It sounds nuts, I know, but Jesus accepted me on those terms and *appeared to me!* He told me He knew I'd never accept Him any other way, so He showed me the man I would wed in my dreams, binding my heart to his in a way that eventually sparked saving faith.

"He knew how alone I felt all my life, so He provided Allen to be my companion, using him as bait to draw me to Himself. The master Fisher of men had my number, offering me an irresistible morsel I couldn't refuse."

She peered at Gina, who was grinning knowingly.

"That was my glimpse into the spirit realm. What you saw was creepy; I wish you could see Jesus, like I did. I never felt so completely accepted before that encounter. He paid for my sins, for all our sins," she waved her hand around the room, taking in the audience, "on the cross so He could share eternity with us.

"Everyone is born into sin and automatically disqualified from His holiness, but now He has reconciled us to Himself through His blood sacrifice. I can't convey how personal it is for Him! We're not numbers. He yearns for you and me individually, intensely, in spite of our hang-ups."

Glancing at Allen, Coop said, "Well, I noticed He let you keep the bait!"

This caused laughter, and Allen colored slightly.

Erin smiled at her guy and took his hand, "Yep, but not without direction. I was charged with comforting him.

Allen came with a broken heart. Jesus is allowing me to assist Him in binding it up."

Coop's gaze shifted to Allen questioningly.

Allen replied, "Our marriage is Erin's first, but not mine. My first ended with a finalized divorce decree one month before we met. She left me three years earlier for greener pastures, I guess. The decree was two months shy of 38 years."

"Whoa!" Gina sat up. "That's rough!"

"Yeah. If not for Erin, I think I would have withered away."

She gripped his hand firmly.

"I had no idea comfort could be administered so aggressively," he gave her a wry smile, "but I don't know if I would have responded to a more gentle approach. Depression is hard to hold onto when someone is rocking your world!"

There was laughter in the crowd.

Erin reminded him with an amused smile, "Hey, I told you sadness was not going to be a way of life for you any more, that I wouldn't allow it, remember?"

"Yes, I do," he confessed. "Thank you."

She gave him a single nod.

"So Jesus wasn't just intervening on my behalf because he favored your prayers?" Gina pinpointed.

"What did the angel tell you?" Allen answered her question with another. "They wanted you to receive salvation, wanted to see you obtain it, you said."

She nodded, adding, "He had a big grin on his face when he said it, too."

"Remember what Fran said at the restaurant?" he went on. "They rejoice to see one sinner saved. They have no relationship with you, so your benefit alone doesn't explain their joy. They bask in their Master's joy, celebrating what pleases Jesus!

"HE KNOWS YOU, even though you don't know Him.

He wanted to come to your rescue, but you never acknowledged Him before, so His hands were tied. He does not violate the will of those who reject Him, but with your life hanging in the balance, He did what He could to gain access on your behalf."

"Huh! This is making sense," Coop blurted out, looking at Gina. "You were in no condition to ask for help, even if you believed in God, which you didn't. So He made use of your voice to get me to call Heidi, knowing she would get these believers praying for you. Without violating your will, He could then answer their prayers. Very clever! He didn't even violate my will, He just persuaded me to call her."

Allen nodded affirmation, "You got it!"

Coop shook his head, "Gina, I didn't see any of what you saw. I'm not convinced God is real, but this explains your recovery when it is otherwise a mystery. I'd like to believe it, I'm just not ready to accept it as real. The idea of an unseen higher power willing to go to such lengths when we need help indicates an extreme care I can't explain. It's an attractive idea, though, I have to admit."

Gina spoke slowly, "I get you, Coop. You're an investigator. You need more evidence, but I know what I saw. I'd be dead if it wasn't real, and that changes things for me."

She turned to Allen, "Jesus saved my life, so whatever I still have going forward is His. I owe Him! Will you lead me to Him?"

Applause broke out. Both agents smiled, and Coop shook his head in disbelief.

Allen started to reply, but Coop cut him off, addressing the room. "You people! I'm not sure if you're fanatics, but you've convinced me of one thing - you care about us!"

The crowd laughed.

"From the bottom of my heart, thank you! It's deeply appreciated."

"That's no mystery, either, if you think about it," Allen told him. "We serve God, too, somewhat like those angels, so what matters to Him matters to us. Prayer on your behalf invested us in seeking your well-being. so we share in His love for you.

"His love, by the way, stems from creating us. We took a wrong turn when we gave into sin, but our existence is His responsibility. He has to judge the sin, but He suspended the sentence to make a way for us to receive redemption. The cost was paid in Jesus' blood, so anyone who trusts in Him can survive the curse of sin! He longs to welcome us home, instead.

"You're not ready to receive Jesus now. Okay, but get used to the idea we will all be praying for the day you will be! We care about you too much to stop, so put that in your pipe and smoke it!" Allen grinned and the rest laughed, nodding in agreement.

He turned to Gina, "It will be my honor to introduce you to Christ. Are you ready?"

She nodded. Bowing their heads, they prayed.

Lord Jesus, I am a sinner. Having learned You died for my sins on the cross, I come to you asking Your forgiveness. Please save me and cleanse me of my guilt and shame. From this day forward, I will live to please You. Help me, I pray, to make You proud until I see Your face! Thank You for loving and redeeming me. I am Yours forever, my God and my King!

Applause mingled with praise filled the room. A flash of bright white light reminiscent of a flashbulb without the pop startled everyone, along with a whoosh of air that swirled momentarily.

Seeing the bewildered looks around him, Allen hazarded his best guess as to what happened, addressing Gina, but loud enough so all could hear, "I think those two angels left in a hurry so they could tell their brethren what they just witnessed! Fran called it. You just made their day, and they wanted you to know!"

Joyous laughter melted into more praise. Coop looked confused and shook his head in wonder.

Gina laid a hand on his arm, "Coop, this is real! A load I never knew I was carrying lifted off me. My heart is lighter than it's ever been. I'm not responsible for *everything* anymore. I just wanted you to know, that's all. I'll be praying with them for you until you understand."

He nodded, "I know. If our places were reversed, I'd do the same for you."

Congratulations started coming her way, then the gathering began to break up. Coop was told over and over it was a pleasure meeting him until he knew they weren't uttering niceties; he could see they meant it. When Gina asked if he minded staying a little longer, he didn't object. He felt quite comfortable.

The numbers dwindled down considerably. Besides the two agents, Allen, Erin, Laurie and Danielle remained, along with Carlos and Juanita. It didn't get awkward until Dani addressed Coop, not the least bit shy.

"Agent Cooper, my heart goes out to you."

His head tilted curiously, uncertain what she meant.

"Everything you two have endured the last few days has required you to stand strong. Gina was struggling to survive, but you took on responsibility when she was incapacitated. You're still carrying that load, trying to help when she isn't one hundred percent."

Gina regarded him thoughtfully. He said nothing, his face expressionless.

"It has to be a strain, so I'll make you an offer," Dani concluded. "It occurs to me you might welcome a workout in the form of a physical challenge. Would you be interested in wrestling me?"

CHAPTER 29

The other ladies grinned, but the guys were shocked!
Coop burst out laughing, "Are you kidding?"

"Not at all," Dani assured him. "I do this for a living, so I don't kid about it. If you accept my offer, I will do my best to force your submission. I'm a veteran with Erin's company and don't intend to lose. I plan to win, so you had better take me seriously!"

Gina warned her, "Coop is trained for law enforcement, but there is something you should know. He is an alternate who is called on to teach new staff occasionally on suspect management and restraint techniques. I don't think you know what you're getting into!"

Dani regarded him coolly, never taking her eyes off him, "That's good to know. The offer stands."

Coop looked at her curiously, "You know, seeing your confidence, I'm tempted."

Gina tried again, "Dani, he doesn't go easy on women. Agency policy prohibits it, because regardless of gender, we face the same dangers."

"I understand. As long as we stick to grappling, I'm not worried," Dani replied. She turned to Allen, "This is where I was asking for your support, yesterday. Will you all watch and give me moral support?"

Allen had a pained expression. He glanced at Laurie before answering, "Dani, I can't."

Dani looked confused, finally uncertain.

Laurie caught Allen's look her way. "Sis, I got this. He's worried about hurting my feelings. Dad, can I speak to you and Mom privately for a minute?"

Allen and Erin rose together to follow her to another room.

She turned and hugged him impulsively before speaking, "I love you so much! That my feelings matter to you means the world to me! But this is okay. You watched my routine, remember? All I ever wanted was to make you proud of me, and you gave me the chance. Mom was right about me. I wanted to show off for you and I did, just not in wrestling. I'm satisfied with what I got.

"Dani's different. The Lord put her up to this for some reason. Knowing her, she'll tell us pretty quickly, but she needs us now. She's all business on the mats, Dad. It will be over almost as soon as it starts. Don't worry about her getting hurt, either. She'll kick his butt!"

He looked at Erin questioningly.

She read his mind, "Your other concern isn't an issue, Sweet Talker. Laurie's assessment is right on the money. Dani will end this so fast, the only reaction you'll have time for is shock! It's Coop who doesn't understand what he's getting into. What she's really doing is getting his attention for whatever she has to say afterward."

That made sense, Allen reflected. She told them there was something she had to do and to say. Considering her anointing as a prophetess, that could be interesting!

He gathered both ladies in his arms, "Okay, I bow to

your wisdom, both of you. Thank you for talking sense to me."

As they broke, he reached out with a finger to lift Laurie's chin. "Young lady, you make me proud of you all over again!"

She beamed as they headed back to their guests.

He whispered to Erin, "Please stay close. This may give me a heart attack!"

She chuckled and took his arm in both of hers reassuringly. Dani's eyes met his as they entered.

With a smile, he told her, "Laurie is very persuasive. I'm here for you."

A big grin lit her face as she turned to face Coop. "If you're inclined to my invitation, we have clothes you can borrow for the match, a good variety to pick through. You don't have to mess up your street clothes."

"How about a shower?" he inquired.

"Out by the pool," came the reply.

"Okay, why not? It's been more than a week since I sparred. You read me right. I've built up more tension than I like, so a workout sounds like fun. Let's see what you have to wear."

Laurie led him to a closet, while Dani went to change.

Erin guided everyone to one of the studios, bringing folding chairs to accommodate them all. Dani came in wearing stretchy yoga pants and a matching halter top. Coop arrived in Hawaiian-style shorts and a T-shirt. He wanted to know the rules.

Dani rattled off, "This is wrestling. No striking or kicking. Biting, hair-pulling, pinching, eye-gouges and scratching are unacceptable and will be met with the same, so let's not go there. Judo holds, throws and chokeholds are okay. Submissions, pins and knockouts win falls.

"The match is conceded verbally or by refusal to stand up to the opponent, which is understood as ending the match. If a knockout occurs, the opponent will wake the sleeper so he can decide whether he wants to continue the match. Any questions?"

"Wow! No, that's fairly thorough. You really are a pro, aren't you?" he noted.

She just smiled. "Ready? Go!"

Both hunched down, warily looking for an opening. He swiped at her once, only meeting air. She mirrored his movement a moment later, but was slow pulling her arm back. He grabbed it, then she grabbed his wrist and fell backward, pulling him down onto a rising foot that thrust him over her body in a spectacular monkey flip! He landed hard on his back, the wind knocked out of him.

To his credit, he tried to sit up even before regaining his breath. It didn't work. Lying on the mat, she spun without getting up, so his rise was interrupted by a knee dropping around his neck like a lariat.

His head was yanked back down onto her other thigh, her leg pinched around his neck like a nutcracker - with his head as the nut! Her leg bulged with muscle that wasn't visible normally, but looked brutal now. Her lower leg bent to fold over her upper ankle, cinching in the hold. Stretching backward, she gripped the ankle of the reinforcing leg to tighten the lock even more.

"Nnngg," he made a choking sound, his mouth unable to move.

"You're done. Tap or nap!" she delivered the ultimatum clearly.

Allen gripped Erin's hand tightly. He had been in this hold more than once, but Erin was gentle, notching it up by degrees until he tapped. He knew it was inescapable. Dani was frightening, pouring on the pressure with what looked to be every ounce of her strength!

Erin watched him with concern and patted his wrist, "It's okay, love. She's just making her point beyond any doubt, that's all."

There was very little struggle. A pained moan of

frustration came from Coop, then he tapped. Dani released him immediately and stood. He sat up slowly, his eyes still glassy. She offered him a hand up, but he shook his head, warding her off with his own.

Gina was agog, "Are you okay?"

He nodded shakily, "I will be, in a minute or two. She wasn't exaggerating. I was on the verge of passing out."

He looked at Dani, "No hard feelings, I just want to sit still and get my bearings before I stand. Sorry to stop so quickly, but I'm not at my best anymore. You win."

Dani smiled good-naturedly and sat cross-legged before him, in easy reach. "Understandable. It's no fun to stand up and fall down again."

"I've never seen anyone take you down so fast," Gina observed.

Coop grimaced, looking Dani in the eye. "She's good, possibly the best I've ever faced. I have to believe she is, because I don't want to think my skills have slipped that badly."

Erin spoke, "Gina, how often do your agents spar like this in a month, and how long are the sessions?"

The reply came, "Depending on how busy we are, two to three hours every other week. Why?"

Dani grinned, "For us, we average a little more than thirty hours weekly. For me, multiply that by eleven years; as I said, I'm a veteran with the company. This is all we do! We're hand-to-hand specialists. You're investigators with side training necessary for your primary job, closing cases. Restraining the subject is your focus, while we intend to break his will by forcing submissions.

"We have different jobs, that's all. In friendly competition, we're hard to beat, but in a life-threatening confrontation, you're probably better prepared to deal than we are."

Erin reassured Coop, "You're not slipping. Your technique was good and your recovery after being thrown was remarkable, but police aren't prepared to take on a full-time gladiator. That pretty much describes who we are."

"Well, I didn't get much exercise, but I learned something new," Coop smiled, apparently recovered by this time. "Any chance of a rematch someday?" he asked Dani.

"We usually charge, but in your case, I'm good with it. You're not gonna win then, either," she teased. "I'll have fun kicking your butt, though. Are you still tense?"

"Huh?"

"You didn't get much exercise, but are you as tense as you were before?" she probed.

He considered a moment, then looked surprised, "No, I'm actually quite relaxed now. How strange!"

With a Cheshire cat grin, she marked an imaginary scorecard in the air with a finger and stated, "Mission accomplished!"

It generated a round of laughter.

"Now I can explain my other reason for challenging you."

CHAPTER 30

Dani continued, "Allen can describe this better than I can." Looking at him, "Please jump in if you see I need help, okay?"

He smiled and gave her a single nod.

"I haven't been saved very long, but after it happened, Jesus began to manifest spiritual gifts in us new converts. In my case, He shows me things like visions and tells me what He wants me to know. It's hard to put it into words."

Allen volunteered briefly, "She is anointed as a prophetess."

Coop's and Gina's eyes widened in surprise.

"I saw you both in visions before we met today. He showed me how you would receive Him, and you weren't ready yet," she looked at Gina and Coop respectively. "Because of your reticence, He indicated I needed to earn your respect before telling you what He showed me."

That was aimed at Coop. She shrugged, "The only way I knew was to defeat you in competition!"

He stood and offered her a hand up from the mat,

which she accepted. He admitted with a bemused smile, "It worked! Even if I don't agree with what you say, believe me, I'll take you seriously! Let's get more comfortable, okay?"

She nodded and they found chairs. He checked on Gina, who said she was not too uncomfortable, and both went quiet,

"The first thing I saw was a closed door. It had a sign on it that read, 'Training.' Quite a few people in casual clothes went in. After a while, they came back out wearing the dark suits your agents wear. They each carried a toolbox they held with pride, as if it were a prized possession. Something else stood out about them, though. Every last one of them was fitted with blinders to block peripheral vision, like horses wear, but they didn't seem to notice! It was weird how they could wear them without knowing they were there.

"The Lord spoke to me then and said to tell you He is removing the blinders placed on you without your permission. When you return to work, you will see things as they are and notice details you formerly overlooked. However, your superiors can't help noticing your blinders are missing and will isolate you. You will not be partners anymore, but they will not tell you upfront, letting it become self-evident over time.

"Gina, you will be assigned to a desk, ostensibly removed from field duty while your leg heals. Once the cast comes off, though, I saw you chained to that desk permanently. You weren't happy, but the Lord will use your position to reveal secrets concerning the inner workings of your agency. What you learn will disgust you, because the agency is hopelessly corrupt."

The studio was dead silent.

She went on, "I saw a red phone in an office marked 'Director.' It was a hotline with two lines and no other buttons. One was clear, labeled POTUS. The other was red with the letters FRB. Orders came to the Director via both lines, but the red line had precedence.

"Coop, you were chained to a flagpole waving the American flag, but it wasn't in America. It seemed like a foreign country with a lot of desert. Instead of getting a new partner, you were given a watchdog that only seemed interested in watching YOU!

"Your placement was intended to keep you out of your superiors' way, and it was also permanent. Your badges doubled as keys that could set you both free from your chains, but they would be used up and destroyed in the process. By the time you decide to release yourselves, you will do so gladly and without regret, having a new direction."

She went silent, having finished.

Gina shook her head, "So that's what prophecy sounds like, huh? It kind of gives me chills, but it'll do more than that if it comes true! I expect desk duty while I recover; nothing far-fetched about that, but the rest... What do you think, Coop? I trust you. It will bum me out if they split us up."

"I agree, but we've known we could be reassigned all along. That's not a stretch, either." His face showed no emotion as he gazed intently at Dani. "I fully respect you, for the record, enough to be completely honest. Your visions sound screwy to me! They're very specific, though, so it will become obvious whether they are accurate.

"The Bureau is my career. It does a lot of good - I don't believe it's corrupt. If my perspective has been obstructed by invisible 'blinders', I guess a new awareness of things previously overlooked might give your words credence.

"I think you're overly imaginative. If you turn out to be right, the world we're familiar with will be turned on its head!"

Gina shook her head, thinking, "You're right, but what I saw has already turned things upside down for me."

He conceded the point with a nod.

She turned to Allen and Erin, "I will need some support with my new beliefs. If her predictions are right, I won't even have Coop near me. Being too alone is unhealthy. What can I do?"

Erin grinned, "You're not alone. Jesus is with you now. He will never leave you nor forsake you. That's His promise to each of us. You have us now, too."

Emphatic nods around the room backed her claim.

"We have daily fellowship via a conference call. Allen covers some scripture, we worship, visit and pray together. Sometimes there are two calls, if someone can't make the first one due to schedule conflicts. It's our lifeline, our protection from being too isolated and what holds us together. We pray for each other, too. Even the most independent among us can't survive as an island.

"I'll give you our numbers and need yours to facilitate this."

Gina gave hers immediately, also recording what Erin provided.

Allen addressed Coop, "You may not have accepted our beliefs today, but I hope you consider us friends. We care about you."

He smiled, "I know. You're good people."

"Thank you," Allen replied. "It's nice to hear. I'm concerned for you, though. I believe Dani heard from God. I know her and I know my Lord; everything she said sounds legit to me."

He glanced at Dani, inclining his head. She smiled at his endorsement.

"If I have it all straight and things come to pass as she foresaw, Gina will be kept where your bosses can watch her, and the Lord will cause the strategy to backfire. He will reveal their secrets, instead! She is under His protection now as one of His own, so she'll be okay.

"You're not automatically protected, though, because

you haven't surrendered to Him. He won't force His will on you, remember?"

"I follow you," Coop replied. "What's your point?"

Allen sat back, his hands folded in his lap, "Just this; if you are cast off into a foreign land, it sounds like you will fall out of favor with those same bosses. Why else would they want you out of their sight? Pairing you up with a watchdog indicates they don't trust you, as well. That would have to rankle, when you've invested your life into the agency snubbing you."

Coop's eyebrows lifted, "You're reading a lot into this, Allen."

"As I said, I take Christ and Dani seriously. Does my logic sound flawed?"

He chewed on it for a moment, "No."

Carlos spoke up, "Coop, Mr. Allen is the most insightful man I know. His insights led me to trust in Christ! I told him once the things he said were like the voice of God speaking to me. I know him lots better now, but being familiar with him hasn't changed my opinion. He's still the wisest man I know!"

Coop seemed impressed.

Allen looked at Carlos, "Wow! Thank you!"

The reply came with a grin, "You know me, Mr. Allen. I just tell it like I see it."

Nodding, Allen turned back to Coop, "Anyway, if it pans out to be true, you'll be more isolated than Gina. Our prayers will join your partner's on your behalf. She warned you about that, remember?"

Coop chuckled as Gina smiled.

"You have friends here that care about you. I want to invite you to sit in on our conference calls whenever you like. Think of it as visiting church, but more personal, since you know the people there. When you don't know who to trust, familiar faces can provide a sense of relief."

"Attending church isn't my cup of tea, but the offer is

thoughtful," Coop replied. "I might do that, knowing Gina's there. It would be good to see how she's doing."

She snorted, "Even if you're reassigned, I expect to hear from you more often than that!"

He cracked up laughing.

"If I'm stuck in the home office and never hear from you, I'll... I'll make sure your paycheck gets lost!"

Several eyes went wide. "Oh!" and "Uh-oh!" came from those listening.

Coop responded hurriedly, "Don't do that! I'll call, I promise! The last thing I need is payroll problems. Sheesh!"

It brought laughter from those present and put a triumphant smile on Gina's face.

Carlos spoke up again, "Mr. Allen, I'd like to hear your take on Dani's visions. Can you clarify any of it for us?"

Things went quiet again.

Allen was hesitant, "Some, maybe. Dani, if I expound on what you saw, will you correct me if you think I'm going the wrong way with it? God gave this stuff to you for a reason. I didn't see it, so I don't have your insight. I don't want to mess up its meaning, if that makes sense. By the way, nothing you said hit me as wrong or unbiblical. As far as I can tell, you did good."

A bright smile lit her face. "Thanks. This kind of thing is still new to me. I didn't want to mess up. Like Carlos, I want to hear your take on it, too. I'll let you know if it seems different from my understanding."

"Okay. God uses symbolism quite a bit in visions - not everything is literal. Obviously, the FBI doesn't use physical blinders on its agents, or we'd see them. You folks would see them," that was addressed to their new friends, who smiled.

"Something in your training conditions you to overlook what you would question otherwise. The blinders are spiritual. That's not accidental. It indicates the use of psychology to affect agents' discernment of right and wrong, which is an occult practice. Something akin to witchcraft is mixed into your basic training."

There was a distinct intake of breath among his listeners. Gina shook her head slowly, while Coop gazed at Allen intently.

He continued, "If God is removing your blinders, He's breaking a spiritual bondage foisted on you without your knowledge. We know from scripture Jesus does that kind of thing. He said of Himself, *Whom the Son sets free is free indeed.*

"Coop, you're not obligated to believe this at all. Either your observations will take on a broader range than before, or they won't. You'll know when you begin to form questions about your agency's operations you've never asked before.

"It will also cause your superiors to realize your conditioning has been undone. They won't like it, but I suspect you'll have no desire to withdraw your questions, either. You strike me as a conscientious and honorable man who won't let reasonable questions be dismissed."

Gina nodded, "You're right. My partner is all that and an investigative bulldog, too. He's been a model for me. I've learned a lot from him."

Coop sat back, surprised. "I didn't know you thought of me that way, Gina. Thanks!"

Allen continued, "Your persistence may be the reason you fall out of favor with your bosses, Coop. The Bureau may have been your idea of your future, but God will remove the veil so you can see what it's really all about. You may decide you are not compatible with what you see and choose a new direction."

"This fits with what I saw, Allen. When he gave up his badge and walked away, he had no regrets. He seemed to be at peace," Dani confirmed.

Coop looked at her, "You know, even though you

kicked my butt and told me things I find hard to swallow, I can't help liking you!"

Dani, Laurie, Juanita and Carlos got a good laugh from it.

Allen added, "Being chained to a desk and a flagpole was symbolic, too. It just indicates the agency will not permit you to grow beyond those assignments. The FBI is not your future, and all the reasons why will be exposed to you before you decide to leave it.

"The watchdog she saw is also a symbol, not really a dog. It will be a new partner who is less than trustworthy, reporting on your activities and attitude."

Coop looked like he had just bit into a sour lemon.

"The image of a dog may also indicate this person is particularly vile, in some way."

"That's pretty thorough, Mr. Allen," Carlos commented. "We'll definitely be praying for both of you." That was directed toward Gina and Coop, who thanked him. "Is there anything else?" he asked Allen.

The older man nodded, "One more thing. It's not a small one. The hotline on the Director's desk has dire implications. The FBI is supposed to be a part of the government's executive branch, loyal and accountable to the United States President. That's why one line was marked 'POTUS.'

"NO ONE ELSE outside his direct chain of command should be giving them orders, but the second line is a clear indication their loyalty has been compromised."

"By who?" Coop demanded, outraged.

"I don't know the individual's name," Allen replied, "but they're working under the auspices of the unofficial fourth branch of government, completely outside the provisions of the U.S. Constitution. FRB is the abbreviation for the Federal Reserve Bank."

CHAPTER 31

"If it's true what you're saying, Allen, that's high treason," Gina admonished him.

"I'm just extrapolating on the vision, guys. I didn't send it. Dani delivered it to us, but she didn't create it, either," he pointed out.

"Nothing is hidden from God. If He removes your blinders to reveal something, it's noteworthy. Showing off is beneath Him. He hates secrets, though, dragging the works of darkness into the light for all to see. You may be who He has chosen to use in this matter."

"Wow! Wow." Coop looked at Gina. "One thing's for sure; our eyes and ears are going to be wide open as we go back to work. If this turns out to be true, it would take divine intervention to expose it and get us through it alive. I'LL bow to Him, in that case!"

His gaze landed on Allen, "If it's not true, I never want to hear about God again."

Allen bowed his head before replying, "Understandable. Whatever happens, we'll be praying for you until you tell us to stop. It's the least we can do."

The younger folks seemed taken aback. Erin laid a hand on his knee and gave it a reassuring squeeze. Covering it with his own, he managed a wan smile. Coop changed his clothes, then he and Gina said goodbye and departed. The remaining group resettled in the living room.

As soon as they were gone, Juanita accosted him, "Mr. Allen, what just happened? Jesus has been here with us this whole time, yet our time together seemed to end on a sour note. I don't understand why."

He roused himself from his somber mood for her sake, managing a weak smile.

"You want to know something? I'm very fond of you, you and Carlos both, actually."

They grinned.

She replied, "We know, Mr. Allen. We love you, too."

He inclined his head in acknowledgment.

"Coop doesn't believe what he heard here today. He's playing a game of life and death with his eternal future, not realizing what's at stake. His last statement was hard to hear! I shouldn't let it get to me, though. As he sees the vision fulfilled, his unbelief is going to slam into a brick wall!

"The Lord will bring him to faith in time, but like his match with Dani, he's gonna have a rough time of it. I feel for him! I guess I ought to focus on the outcome. It will be worth it in the end."

Erin took his hand and smiled encouragingly when he looked at her.

"Sweet Talker, he survived that match!"

There were giggles as he smiled.

"It was a rude awakening, but I had the impression he didn't regret it, even though he lost. I don't think we've seen the last of him."

Dani agreed, "I don't think so, either."

She turned red as Erin added, "Besides, you heard

what he said. He likes her!"

The other girls lit up, looked at their veteran coworker and went, "Ooooo!"

Her red shade went brighter as she protested, "Hey, I didn't do anything..."

The protest faded into something incomprehensible. A tiny smile formed as the redness faded. Apparently, the idea didn't distress her too much.

Gina and Coop hardly spoke on the way to the hotel where they were staying. Both seemed lost in their thoughts. When he asked how she was feeling, she admitted she was tired and looked forward to lying down. Her face was still swollen from the cuts and bruises she sustained in the collision. Thinking back on what happened, he was amazed she survived at all!

When they arrived, she had a message to contact their medical division Monday morning before traveling. Neither knew what it was about, but supposed it would become clear when she called. She said she'd be ready to eat after a nap, then stretched out on her bed, still fully clothed. That's when he became talkative.

"I guess I shut Allen down at the end of the visit," he mused. "Do you think I was rude or offended him?"

"A little rude, yes." She was slightly annoyed at his timing, but didn't really mind. "Was he offended? No, I think he was worried about you. You may not believe in God, but he certainly does. You all but threw down the gauntlet for God to prove Himself! What could Allen say? The only thing he could say was they would keep praying for you.

"Now I have a question. Considering how strong your choice of words was, were *you* offended at either him or God?"

He thought it over, "Maybe. Allen's been nothing but welcoming and supportive of us here. Only a fool could resent that, but his certainty in his beliefs is unsettling. I don't know how I can rationally take offense at a being I don't accept as real, though, so hostility toward God wouldn't be sane."

"Are you sure about that?" she challenged. "You heard the same gospel I did. God holds us accountable for going our own way, calling it sin. He declares us unilaterally guilty of abandoning our Creator and says we will burn in hell for rejecting Him - UNLESS we accept His Son Jesus' sacrifice as the substitute for our own.

"That came through loud and clear! I did accept it, but I can see how someone who doesn't could take offense. You may not be sure whether He's real, but His claims could still offend you. No one likes to be told he's been wrong all his life!"

With a sour look on his face, he replied, "You're making sense."

"You've got a problem, partner," she pointed out. "You're faced with unanswered questions. As an investigator, you don't like those. They're upsetting your organized little world, not fitting into your worldview because you didn't accept the explanations Allen supplied I did, so I have peace, also having made peace with God on His terms.

"What happened to me? How did prayer by some likable fanatics turn things around for us, for me? Did I imagine what I told you I saw? Is your partner losing her marbles?"

Smiling, he shook his head.

She acknowledged, "I appreciate you're trusting me, but my vision has to make you wonder where it originated.

"Who told you to call Heidi, if it wasn't me? I'm here with you now because you did! Thank you, by the way. Lastly, the flash and swirl of air when I received Christ... What was that? A mass hallucination? More than twenty people witnessed it, because they talked about it afterward.

You have your work cut out for you, if you plan to find answers other than those you heard.

"You could have asked God to show you He's real when I prayed, but not you!" She grinned, "No, you slapped Him in the face and told Him to put up or shut up. I don't think Allen took it personally. However, taking God seriously, he was worried when you didn't. In his eyes, you poked a bull and risked getting the horns, sort of like you're doing now by keeping me awake!"

He grinned, "Sorry. I'll let you sleep. Thanks for your input."

Erin sent out dinner plans to all their friends, inviting them to meet together at a quarter to six. With a couple of hours to kill, the younger folks wanted to swim and talked Erin and Allen into joining them. The couple went to change in their room.

Allen tightly embraced her. She asked why he was so quiet. Still in each other's arms, he looked her in the eye and told her earnestly, "Thank you."

"For what?" She had no idea what he was talking about.

"My Lord! Dani flattened Coop like he was nothing! The guy has to know how to take care of himself, but he didn't stand a chance against her; and according to everyone here, you're better than she is. I know you take it easy on me, but had no clue how much you were holding back for my sake. Seeing what she did drove it home today. Honestly, it was frightening to see! Thank you -"

She cut him off, placing a finger on his lips, "Sweet Talker, you don't have to thank me. I can't hurt you! The thought itself is painful to me. You trust me, so hurting you is off-limits, even when I feel ornery. No way will I betray your trust!

"I'm content to force a few playful submissions and jump your bones." She gave him a sly look, resulting in a grin. "After this morning's preparations nearly went off the rails, you can bet I'll finish what we started tonight!"

He kissed her invitingly. She backed up, breaking the embrace, and shook her head with a smile.

"Tonight, love! Your teasing will come back to haunt you! For now, let's go get wet with the kids."

The activity was relaxing and also strengthened the bond with the younger folks. It came out that Juanita was self-conscious of her appearance. Allen couldn't see why; if her condition was showing in the slightest, he couldn't tell.

The other ladies were supportive, reminding her it would be worth it in the end. It seemed to help. Carlos thanked them, pointing out that his reassurances tended to be dismissed as "just trying to make her feel better."

Allen reflected back on his experiences long ago. Sometimes a guy is at a disadvantage, when his encouragement is disregarded, no matter how sincere - but if he says something wrong, it will follow him to his grave!

Remembering this, he advised Carlos to keep encouraging her, but minimize his words in favor of listening. Guys can't fix everything for their loved ones. Sometimes, they shouldn't try. It's enough to stand by the one in need.

"Hugs speak volumes, too, when words just don't seem to matter," Erin added, her arm going around her husband. "This man taught me that without ever speaking a word! I never felt so loved before meeting him. A woman can overlook a lot of verbal blunders when she knows he means well."

Allen looked at her questioningly.

She answered, "No, you've done pretty well, Sweet Talker. Nothing needs to be redressed between us. You've built up a lot of credit with me, so if you ever do trip up, you'll be in good shape. I know your heart's in the right place."

"Same here," Juanita told Carlos, grasping his hand.

"Sorry if your words don't immediately have the effect you want. My moods are hard to shake, but I get through them because you're near. You're gonna make a great dad!"

A smile lit his face as he seemed to breathe a sigh of relief.

CHAPTER 32

I t amazed Allen when nearly everyone in their fellowship joined them for dinner in the evening. The bond the Lord had created between all of them boggled him! Fran was working and Reina didn't make it, but most of the rest were there. An invitation went out to Gina and Coop, but they passed, citing a need for rest. They gathered in a Mexican restaurant with a room opened just for them. Their number made such arrangements preferable so they could hear each other without disturbing other customers.

It gave them time to enjoy visiting without an agenda. Between the wedding and events centering around their new friends in the FBI, Allen and Erin hadn't had much free time during this visit. It was nice to catch up.

Eli was taking some time to step back and consider his options before committing to a new education plan. Allen and Ted agreed it was a good choice, with Allen pointing out the importance of presenting his thoughts to the Lord in prayer. Eli assured him he was already doing so.

Laurie filled them in on what took place at the house

EXPOSING HIDDEN WORKS OF DARKNESS

after Gina's salvation. Dani's vision had made an impression on her, it seemed. Her respect for her wrestling mentor was growing as she saw how God was using her in new ways!

Eli expressed his disappointment to Dani. "I would have liked to see you take Coop down!"

Allen came back instantly, "No, you wouldn't! I was there. I nearly jumped out of my hide!" There were laughs, but he was serious. "It's one thing to hear how good these ladies are at what they do, but it's downright scary to see it happen in front of you. I'm proud of Dani's expertise, but I'm in no hurry to risk a heart attack by seeing it again!"

Dani looked at him with concern.

Erin rested a hand on his forearm, "He's good, just got a shock, that's all. Being exposed to a normal day for us would be like riding the world's biggest roller coaster for him. You made an impression on more than just Coop!"

"I'll be okay," he told Dani, then turned to Eli. "That horseshoe Laurie gave you? Imagine *you* were the horseshoe, instead."

The teen winced.

"Yeah, Being bent out of shape or crushed senseless isn't fun, even if it's a gorgeous woman doing it. Guys who think it is are brain-damaged! I'll go to my grave convinced of that," he glanced toward Erin with a smile, "but if she shows you mercy, the pain is quickly forgotten."

Ted's focus was elsewhere. "Allen, the Federal Reserve... The idea they're pulling the FBI's strings is unsettling. If it's true they command more influence than the President, then our government is way off-balance! How can it be fixed?"

Worried expressions confronted the older man. He wished he could offer comfort.

"For us, it's just not possible, Ted. I have no doubt it's true. No matter how noble its goals appear to be, a federal banking system is at its heart a power grab. It was attempted way back in the 1820s, when the nation was less than forty years old, so the aim isn't new. President Andrew Jackson was an old war horse who fought it tooth and nail over both his terms. Those wanting it fought dirty, plunging the country into a deep recession and creating unnecessary suffering to get their way. It's all they cared about!

"The effort was finally defeated, more than six years after it started. When President Jackson retired, a journalist asked him what he considered his greatest accomplishment in office. He replied, "I killed the bank!" He was a hero who led us to victory in the War of 1812, yet he considered a federal bank system to be a greater threat to the nation than an invasion! That speaks volumes.

"Roughly ninety years later, globalists tried again, but President Woodrow Wilson approved it this time. In 1913, after Congress ended its session to go home and celebrate Christmas, less than a handful of members illegally voted on legislation to create the current Federal Reserve System. It was forwarded without deliberation or opposition to the President, who signed it into law on December 23rd. Most of Congress heard about it in the news, never getting any say in the matter!"

Conrad was shaking his head, but Andrew spoke up first. "That's not accurate according to the history books, Allen. The vote wasn't illegal. A few had left D. C., but eighty-plus senators participated in ratifying the bill. It couldn't have been illegal."

Conrad nodded emphatic agreement.

"Have you heard the axiom, 'history is written by the victors?' Allen replied. "It's not wrong. The records have been altered to avoid legal challenges after the deed was done. Think about it.

"Forty-eight states had elected representatives in Washington. Cross-country travel was largely reliant on trains. Cars were not up to it yet, and there wasn't much in the way of roads, anyway. Planes weren't available. The

Wright brothers invented them less than ten years earlier.

"Has Congress ever inconvenienced themselves for anything short of an emergency?"

Grins were everywhere as heads shook a negative.

"They'd have ended their session with ample time to get home, at least ten days to two weeks. Anyone who remained either had no family to spend the holidays with, or were privately PAID to stay behind. There's a rumor it was carried out by just three members who delivered the bill to the President, which would indicate he was in on it and it was prepared before the break. As a body, Congress had no opportunity to vote on it. That was timed intentionally.

"The whole thing reeks of corruption! The facts don't support the revised history, don't even make sense... and no one cares. It's done, and there's no going back to fix it.

"Jesus declared that *the love of money is the root of all kinds of evil.* That's exactly what's at work here. The Federal Reserve became the national bank to sack the nation - and it succeeded. The national debt, chiefly held by the Bank, is far too big to be collectible; even the interest payments are unrealistic. Like Congress, which votes its members pay raises whenever they like, the FRB sets interest rates arbitrarily to its liking."

Dani was flabbergasted, "So you think what I saw was right, the red phone, I mean?"

Allen nodded, "Absolutely. Communication may take a different form than an actual red phone, but the symbolism is plain. Jesus showed you the truth of things."

Hans, silent until now, interjected, "This is a powder keg. If our new agent friends uncover it, their lives will be forfeit, unless the Lord protects them."

He looked around at the others meaningfully. "Coop and Gina must be held up in prayer. Your prayers, in agreement with my daughter, saved my life! Now we must champion them before God, for their souls and their lives!"

Allen applauded. Erin joined him, followed by the rest. He told Hans, "I couldn't have said it better myself! Shall we pray?"

Heads bowed around the room.

"Heavenly Father, we come before You in Jesus' name. Thank You for our new friends and for Gina's salvation. Please draw Coop to You as well; we claim him for Your kingdom so he won't be lost. As we've studied what you revealed to us through Dani, we're concerned for their safety. The wicked have secrets they guard jealously, but nothing is hidden from You. Please protect them as you unveil mysteries and strip away the darkness in which the Devil's minions try to hide.

"You are the Revealer of secrets. Be glorified as You work to establish true justice, not the phony justice that condemns the righteous and enriches those in power. Give Coop and Gina the wisdom, support and resources to navigate this minefield of deception without being harmed. Thank You in advance for hearing and answering our prayers, in Jesus' name. Amen."

Applause broke out among praises.

Hans let out a deep breath, "Whew! No wonder I was saved, with prayers like that going up for me!"

It brought forth chuckles.

"Gina saw angels, and I saw glimpses of one, too, all in response to prayer. I am curious what God might dispatch in answer to this one."

Allen shrugged, "There's no telling. Usually, the help goes unseen. Whatever the case, you can be sure it will be sufficient for the need."

Heads nodded in agreement.

"When are you two going home?" Fran inquired. "Is this our last visit before it happens?"

Erin replied, "We left it open this time. Stef and I have

an offer to sell the company; you may have heard something about it."

Most seemed surprised at the news.

"We're negotiating. It's a good offer. Stef's excited. They want her to stay on and run things, even with buying her out. I'm ambivalent, but it may become too good to pass by. The Lord has hinted the company is part of my past, but not my future. We'll see."

Denise and Alissa looked like they might cry.

Teresa voiced their concerns, "You'll still come to see us, I hope? You and Allen mean the world to us! You two have changed our lives!"

Allen smiled, "Of course we will! It's the Lord who changed all our lives, but we're family now! Honestly, this is the first trip we've made with any motivation about business. EVERY trip after the first one has been about seeing all of *you*. We get excited at the thought of spending time with you! We'll still have daily fellowships, too."

He looked at Erin. "We love being part of your lives and having you in ours."

Tears streaked Alissa's face, but they didn't hide the grin shining through.

He focused on her as he finished, "Even when my daughters are with me in Missouri, I still have to come see my niece, don't I?"

She nodded enthusiastically, giggling.

"And your nephew!" Erik pointed out. "Even if you don't bring gifts, we still want to see you!"

Erin reassured them, "We'll have hugs, regardless."

She sounded a bit choked up to her husband. As dinner wound down, no further plans were made for the evening. Erin needed time to confer with Stef, but hugs were passed out in abundance as they all parted. She held her tears until seated behind the wheel next to Allen, then broke when his arms went around her.

He whispered, "I know. I love 'em, too."

She chuckled, nodding in agreement.

CHAPTER 33

E rin and Allen arrived back at the house to find Stef
in her office. She came out to the living room as
soon as they arrived, an air of resolve about her she
didn't normally carry.

Erin asked how her weekend went.

"More stressful than expected," came the enigmatic
reply. Stef didn't elaborate, choosing to change the subject.

"You know, I've given careful thought to your
inclination to ask for more money. Sleeping on it changed
my perspective, I have to admit. I advised Emily to go with
you because life is short and hesitance leads to regret. If we
didn't up the ante, I'd always wonder what would've
happened if we did. Life IS short, so let's do it!"

Allen laughed. "You told us we might talk you into
this, but it sounds like you did it all by yourself."

Erin cracked up at his observation.

Stef grinned widely, "Yeah, I guess I did. I'm very
stubborn; Erin probably warned you."

Erin immediately nodded, with a chuckle.

"It's bad, when I can't even win an argument with myself! Or maybe I'm just greedy. In any case, what you said is true," looking at Erin. "We're happy as things stand, so if the offer is withdrawn, what have we lost?"

"Well, I know where we stand now," Erin sat back, heaving a sigh. "I wouldn't have pursued more money without your agreement."

"I know," Stef replied. "My investment is considerably less than yours, but you have always treated me like a full partner. You'll never understand how much that means to me! Your respect gives me the confidence to manage this company. Your trust challenges me not to fail you."

Allen grasped his wife's hand, smiling at her proudly. "I never could have successfully pursued this woman," he confided to Stef, "but I made out like a bandit when she chose me!"

Erin blushed.

He continued, "We're both blessed to have her as a friend and partner. That's no lie!"

Stef nodded in vehement agreement.

The corners of Erin's mouth turned up slightly before asking, "This is a different approach. Have you two decided to embarrass me, now, in place of ganging up to tease me?"

Allen grinned, while Stef roared with laughter.

After a moment, he declared, "Genie, I am genuinely proud of you, in awe of you, and just the tiniest bit afraid of you! Why would I bait you, knowing your capabilities?" He shook his head. "I'm only speaking the truth. I think you know that. It just puts you on the spot, that's all."

A one-sided smile preceded her response, "You know me too well, Sweet Talker. I love your honesty, and I love you! Thank you both for regarding me so highly. It's mutual. I'm blessed to have you as partners, and that's no lie, either!"

Stef said, "Well, since we've established our own

admiration society, shall we set our new price?"
After the laughter subsided, they did.

Monday morning arrived, and Gina called the Bureau's doctor in Washington D.C. at 8:00 a.m. Pacific Time sharp, as instructed. A likable old fellow, she wondered what was on his mind. It didn't take long to find out.

"Agent Smythe? Thanks for calling. How are you?"

She explained she felt okay, all things considered. He knew her condition from the hospital and Coop's reports, but was following up on her personally. When she told him they expected to book a flight back the same day, he stopped her abruptly.

"Negative," he corrected her. "You are not to board a plane before Thursday, understood?"

It caught her off-guard.

"If you want to take a car or a train, knock yourself out, but you'll have to wait until tomorrow. I'm texting you the name and address of a medical office we use in L.A. An appointment has been made to see you at 1:00 p.m. today. You will be evaluated and get a cast on that leg before they're through. They will prescribe something for pain, too."

Coop, always attentive, watched her closely, seeing her surprise.

"Dr. Watkins, why the no-fly order? I don't get it."

"Agent Smythe, are you familiar with professional wrestling?"

"WRESTLING? What are you talking about?"

Coop indicated she should go to speakerphone. She did so, explaining her partner Agent Cooper wanted to join the call.

"Coop, you old hound, how are you?"

"I'm good, Ira. Trying to help a lame partner back in the saddle. What's this about wrestling?"

No one had reported their experience yesterday,

agreeing it was superfluous. It was the height of irony the doctor was bringing up the subject!

Gina stuck her tongue out at being labeled 'lame'.

Dr. Watkins dissembled, "I've followed pro wrestling off and on most of my life. Years ago, a fellow named Chris Candido suffered a broken ankle, just like your partner. He made a promo appearance on crutches the next day in another state, hopping a short flight to get there, then went home. Shortly after arrival, he collapsed and was hospitalized. Within hours, he was dead at age thirty-six!

"Turned out a blood clot formed near the break. It's normal for that to happen as broken bones start to heal. Clots form, then dissolve naturally over a couple of days, but this man's flight interrupted the natural process.

"The drastic elevation change shook the clot loose. It migrated to his lungs, causing a sudden onset of pneumonia that killed him before he was even diagnosed. I don't want a patient of mine to suffer the same misfortune, so I don't let them fly until 48 hours after casting - *especially* with a broken leg!

"Land travel's okay, but Agent Smythe will be miserable. I advise you to relax and wait for Thursday, then board a plane. The rest will be good for her. Make sense now?"

Gina spoke up, "It sure does! Thanks, Dr. Watkins, for everything. We'll follow your instructions."

"When agents break themselves up, we patch 'em up. It's what we do! Glad to help."

Before he could hang up, Coop's curiosity got the best of him. He blurted out, "Ira, do you know anything about session wrestling?"

There was a short pause before he slowly answered, "Coop, what you do on your own time is none of my business. That sounds personal."

Coop was taken aback. "Huh? No, I don't think so. Gina - Agent Smythe watched!"

Dr. Watkins hesitated, "This doesn't sound like a tryst. Care to explain?"

Gina watched her partner, amused at his predicament.

Coop stated carefully, "We became acquainted with some people at the hospital, then went to visit them yesterday. They said they were session wrestlers. After a while, one of them said I looked tense and offered to wrestle me and exercise some of the tension away."

A huge belly laugh drowned out anything else he might have said. Gina grinned as both waited for the doctor to regain his composure.

When he did, he posed a question, "Did she hand you your head, Coop?"

Gina laughed.

Flustered, Coop objected, "I never said it was a woman!"

Dr. Watkins chuckled, "You didn't have to. There's no market for male session wrestlers, because most women are smart enough not to go looking for trouble the way we do! The few women tough enough to decide challenging men is a good idea can simply *become* session wrestlers, then sit back and let the men come to them. Now answer my question. She beat you, didn't she?"

In a low tone he replied, "Embarrassingly fast! I couldn't even defend myself."

There was more laughter on the line.

Gina joined in the mirth, stating, "Dr. Watkins, the more we talk, the more I like you!"

Coop scowled at her, but she just laughed harder.

The medical man gasped, "I wish I could have seen it."

Coop regretted ever mentioning what happened.

Ira collected himself. "Coop, in wrestling, there are pros, and then there are *pros*. Pro wrestling on TV is made up of stunts executed by people specializing in such things. They're like Hollywood stunt people, following a choreographed routine to present the appearance of competitors striving for victory.

"Truly damaging the opponent would take out the promotion's players, ending the show, so they work together to make it look convincing, then put on another show somewhere else. Injuries do happen because the stunts are risky, but at its heart, it's show business."

"Session wrestlers face amateurs, mostly, so they have to assert dominance early on to control the match and limit injuries. Those they face either agree not to fight back or go all out. That can be dangerous for everyone involved, so the wrestler must take over for safety's sake.

"She takes the offensive from the beginning, picking apart the challenger with submission after submission until the opponent has no fight left in him - or she knocks him out. He's no threat when he's unconscious, and much less of a threat when he wakes up with diminished responses."

Ira was making sense, Coop reflected. He nearly passed out and recognized how it impaired him, so he stopped the match. Good thing he did, too! If Ira was right, continuing would have turned his embarrassing situation into a slaughter.

"Anyone can play-act, though the pros on television are some of the best. They coordinate to put on the show without serious injuries. Session wrestlers don't have anyone to share the responsibility, though, so they have to be good enough to bear it alone.

"They *must* be control freaks on the mats to make sure injuries don't happen, which would be bad for business. Often they give up size, weight and reach advantages to larger opponents, making up for it with experience, flexibility and resilience. Guys have no idea they're up against some of the best grapplers on the planet, pound-for-pound!

"Do you have a rematch planned?"

"Yes, but not scheduled," Coop answered.

"Then allow me to spare you another blow to your ego,

Coop. Cancel it. The mind plays tricks on you, telling you she got lucky. It's not true. She'll clean your clock all over again and laugh at your struggles as she breaks you down.

"She's that good! If you ever have to take one into custody, that's what backup is for. Otherwise, you're liable to end up wearing your own handcuffs... and you certainly don't want her taking your gun away from you!"

"Wow! Thanks for the insight, but I wonder if you might be exaggerating their skills a bit," he mused.

Dr. Watkins snorted, "It's your neck; risk it if you like. Let me give you something else to wonder about. Would these ladies keep competing if they regularly lost? It wouldn't take me long to decide I was in the wrong line of work if I kept getting beat! How about you?"

"No, that would get old fast," Coop admitted wryly. "She was confident when she challenged me, almost to the point of arrogance. That's partly why I accepted her challenge, besides it sounded like fun. I guess that explains her confidence."

"Which was well-founded," Ira pointed out. "I enjoyed the conversation, but I need to get back to work. Agents get some combat training, but it doesn't qualify you as specialists. It's cocky to think you can take on all comers with such training. You got a wake-up call, but at least your life wasn't on the line this time. If you see her again, you should thank her for that!"

The call ended. Moments later, Gina received the text with her appointment details.

CHAPTER 34

E rin received a call about 9:00 the same morning from Fred Bigelow. *He must be enthused about acquiring A*C*E,* she thought to herself. *At least he was courteous enough to wait until I'm up.* It was noon on the east coast.

He greeted her cheerfully before inquiring about their decision. Erin reminded him of the reputation she worked hard to build, something he had told Stef he valued before ever talking to Erin. He readily agreed it was an appealing part of the deal. Erin further pointed out business was good, so she wasn't really motivated to sell, then made her counter offer.

"Ouch! You drive a hard bargain, but for a minute there, I thought you were turning me down flat. Let me review my resources and call you back, okay? It should be in two or three hours."

She agreed and hung up. Allen just waited, watching her.

She shook her head, "You know, I think he's going to

accept it! Looks like we read him right. Stef will be overjoyed if it works out."

He shrugged, "It's in the Lord's hands. It would be wonderful to see her blessed, but truthfully, I'm happy if you're happy. Are you?"

"Yes, however it goes, I think."

She sat on the bed beside him; he hadn't got up yet. He started to rise up, but her hand on his chest pressed him back down.

A mischievous grin met his eyes, "I'm not sure I'm ready to let you up."

His eyes went wide, "Genie, you wiped me out last night! Give me a chance to recharge, okay?"

She leaned down over him, looking him in the eye. "You had all night, Sweet Talker. I told you your teasing would come back to haunt you, so you had fair warning! I'm not greedy, though, so this is what will happen.

"After teasing *you*, I'll let you up. It'll give you something to think about as the day goes by. You said you made out like a bandit because I pursued you. Honey, I'm not done! I will NEVER stop staking my claim on you. You're just gonna have to live with it!"

She did what she said. It was the first time she worked him into a lather without finishing him. When she did let him up, he felt deprived, yet there was a sense of relief at the same time.

He told her it bordered on torture. She laughed, compounding his frustration by flirting with him throughout the day. He was simmering by bedtime!

In the meantime, Mr. Bigelow kept his word. Prepared to accept her offer, he wanted to confirm Stef's willingness to stay on as manager for at least six months. Erin said although she seemed to be pleased with the idea, he would have to finalize the details with her on that point.

He stated he would have his lawyer draw up the sales contract. It wouldn't take long. Erin gave him contact information so her attorney could go over it prior to signing.

Stef was excited. The deal was poised to make her a multimillionaire when complete, skipping the first million she hadn't quite attained yet. Bigelow exceeded her requested salary to stay on, too.

She hugged Erin and offered a hand to Allen, thanking him for the idea of seeking a windfall. He looked at her hand, shook his head and spread his arms. She grinned, gathering him up in a massive bear hug lasting only a moment.

"You guys!" she declared. "I'm never gonna be the belle of the ball, but because of you I've become *somebody*. You two are my only family, you know that? We aren't going to be partners anymore, but please don't exit my life!

"Both of you mean more to me than I can ever express. Sometimes I'm not sure who I am anymore, but you ground me, reminding me I am loved. You are my anchor! Don't become strangers, okay?"

"Never gonna happen, Sis," Erin assured her. "As you said, we're family."

"We've got more than three acres," Allen pointed out. "Why couldn't a rich woman like you buy one, build a vacation home on it and be our neighbor?"

Erin grinned as Stef cracked up laughing.

Spreading his arms, he added, "Consider the possibilities!"

"You've got me thinking, Allen," Stef confessed. "I do know people in Missouri, it's true. If I retire in six months, I'll have to look into my options."

Fred Bigelow was on the phone, reporting the results of his negotiations to his 'silent' partner. *Not really so silent,* he reflected to himself. Purchasing A*C*E was her idea. She had several ideas about the matter she insisted must be implemented. Any attempts to modify them were casually brushed aside in a way that left him no grounds to argue.

It was strange, but he wasn't able to take offense. Acquiring A*C*E was strategically a sound move to expand his business, if the price hadn't become outrageous. He only accepted because his partner agreed to meet it out of her own pocket! She was determined to make the deal, so he agreed.

Disagreeing with her never seemed to work; besides, if he had wondered how determined she was to bring about the merger, the money she was investing laid his questions to rest. Now he wondered if their partnership hadn't formed specifically to acquire A*C*E.

"Yes, ma'am, the junior partner has agreed to manage for a six-month minimum while they transition under our umbrella," he replied. "She asked for an ungodly salary I'd never pay my other employees, but -"

She cut him off, so he listened until she finished.

"Hey, if you're willing to pay it, that's fine by me," he agreed. "She seems quite capable. Their business has flourished since Mrs. Edwards retired -"

He was corrected sharply, cut off again. Something he said angered her.

"Yes, ma'am, I'm fully aware Erin ADAMS built A*C*E," he pointed out slowly. "I know who my competitors are. It never occurred to me you might take offense to her new legal status and name. Please forgive me." *That was bizarre,* he thought. *Does she have an axe to grind with Erin's husband?*

She genuflected, apparently realizing her overreaction. When she expressed her satisfaction with the results of his negotiations, pride swelled in his chest. She seemed to think money was no object. As long as it didn't risk his, she could spend all she wanted! His business was taking a big leap forward, becoming bicoastal, a dream come true. Her investment made it possible. She thanked him.

He shook his head, even though she couldn't see him. "No, thank *you*," he returned. "Going nationwide was something I always wanted to do. Your capital is making it happen, sweetened by Erin's reputation being swirled into the mix. Thank you for your interest. Our partnership is enriching us both, Dame Hilda."

She agreed and hung up.

Silly, useful dolt, she thought to herself with a smile. *I'm enriching myself. When your usefulness is ended, I'll initiate a curse to end YOU, leaving everything in my hands once again!*

Hilda Goins had become a billionaire in exactly this manner, establishing partnerships that ended abruptly when her partners died in ways no one could connect to her. Heidi knew her well and feared her because of it. It was a healthy fear that kept her malleable well past the age other children would strike out on their own.

Then Allen Edwards entered the picture. She often wondered where he came from, to upset her plans so completely? A Missouri nobody Erin Adams fell head over heels for, even receiving Christ after meeting him. It made no sense.

She sent Heidi and Arum to kill him, to no avail. Arum *fled* when he failed, and her daughter... Blood must sometimes be sacrificed to achieve an end. Giving up Heidi was acceptable on those terms, but Heidi was simply pried out of her grasp. The destruction of the Eye of Darkness she bore was proof power exceeding her own was at play!

The Power that protected Allen also covered Heidi now. Hilda cursed Allen when Arum failed. She tried, anyway. It bounced back at her dangerously, nearly killing her. Such a thing had never happened before! Being no novice, she disarmed it, but the message was clear. He and those with him were under protection she couldn't breach.

The leader of the Ascended Masters, the one Christians

called Satan, was who she answered to. He doesn't tolerate failure, and Hilda's were racking up. To save face, she hired Bart Palombo. He was a man, true, but his prowess as an assassin was well-established. He was swatted down before he could get a shot at Heidi, with a finality underscoring how untouchable she had become.

Finally, there was Janet McCullough. Her elimination should have been business as usual, no big deal. Instead, she disappeared as though she never existed. If her identity was an alias, that would explain much and vindicate Hilda's caution in eradicating her, but no report of success returned.

Her constructs were designed to succeed and report before dissipating. It was as if her curse on the woman was erased! THAT never happened before. Hilda's curses were devastatingly effective, at least until A*C*E came into the picture.

Well, there'll be no more of that, she pondered with satisfaction. *No more resurrections or surprises in a cemetery I own! Allen and Erin think they're untouchable, but I'll see to it the plots are filled, starting with Erin Adams' business partner!*

ABOUT THE AUTHOR

L. A. Goodyear is a jack of all trades. He has worked in lumber yards, a donut shop, warehouses, truck driving, cashiering - even participated in laser surgery! A veteran of the U.S. Navy, his most recent occupation was that of a caregiver for the developmentally disabled.

He loves to laugh and get others laughing, but most of all he loves talking about the Lord Jesus he serves. Obeying and spending time with Him is a joy he'd share with everyone, if he could! He sees ministry as a matter of meeting needs whenever enabled to do so by the power of God, rather than an occupation to earn a livelihood, and is acutely aware he will give account for his faithfulness.

L. A. maintains a blog, *thefoolishnessofgod.com*, where he expounds on scripture and sometimes airs his thoughts on matters of interest. He can be reached at *thefoolishnessofgod@yahoo.com*. It amuses him to tell people he writes foolishness! Time will tell if it really is.

www.ingramcontent.com/pod-product-compliance
Lightning Source LLC
Chambersburg PA
CBHW071907220626
47052CB00002B/248

* 9 7 8 1 9 6 4 5 5 9 9 5 7 *